How Ironic That The Spot His Bride Had Chosen For Their Wedding Had Once Been The Most Popular Dueling Ground In New Orleans.

Too bad the twenty-first century was more civilized. If Jake could have called his bride's father out and shot him, he would have.

Jake wanted to hate Alicia for complicating his life, but reason told him he was equally to blame. He didn't want to marry her, but with every word that the priest uttered binding him to Alicia Butler, his desire for her grew until it felt like a crushing weight. Indeed, ever since he'd agreed to the marriage, thoughts of Alicia in his bed had consumed him.

They say a little piece of paper doesn't matter. That it changes nothing.

They don't know anything. He felt trapped. Doomed. At the same time his body raged to have her again.

Dear Reader,

I believe that love is the most powerful positive force in the world and that if we open our hearts, it will find us and change our lives for the better. Not that I think we always get to choose who we love or when we fall in love, but isn't that what makes it so interesting?

After Alicia's wealthy father is accused of embezzlement on a grand scale and arrested, she is devastated. Just when she thinks she's lost everything and has nowhere to turn, she discovers she's pregnant by Jake Claiborne, the man who slept with her and then reported her dad to the feds.

Although she'd rather never see Jake again, she knocks on his door and tells him they're going to have a baby.

Having lost her own mother young, Alicia has always longed to be part of a loving family. Naturally, she wants this for her baby, as well. At first she sees no possibility of realizing her dream in her temporary marriage of convenience to Jake, but slowly, miraculously, she finds ways to build on what they feel for one another until she does.

Enjoy,

Ann Major

ANN MAJOR

ULTIMATUM: MARRIAGE

Published by Silhouette Books

America's Publisher of Contemporary Romance

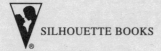 SILHOUETTE BOOKS

ISBN-13: 978-0-373-73054-4

ULTIMATUM: MARRIAGE

Recycling programs
for this product may
not exist in your area.

ANN MAJOR

lives in Texas with her husband of many years and is the mother of three grown children. She has a master's degree from Texas A&M at Kingsville, Texas, and is a former English teacher. She is a founding board member of the Romance Writers of America and a frequent speaker at writers' groups.

Ann loves to write; she considers her ability to do so a gift. Her hobbies include hiking in the mountains, sailing, ocean kayaking, traveling and playing the piano. But most of all she enjoys her family. Visit her Web site at www.annmajor.com.

This book is dedicated to my talented editor,
Krista Stroever.

One

"Sorry, Claiborne. The decision's been made. You're off the project. A lot of people don't like all the notoriety and publicity you've been getting lately because of your association with Mitchell Butler and his daughter, Alicia."

Jake knew better than to defend himself by saying he was a victim of Butler, too.

"I'm just the messenger," the caller said.

Jake clenched the phone but said nothing more. He wouldn't beg.

Not that he hadn't tried to defend himself to the press earlier in the week after they'd set up base camps outside his home and office. All he'd accomplished was to give the reporters words to twist in such a way as to make him look like he was guilty of having been a partner to Butler's embezzlement scheme.

A final click was followed by a dial tone.

For a second Jake thought about Mitchell Butler and his beautiful daughter. Had she aided and abetted her father?

Jake Claiborne felt his headache build as he replaced the telephone. Not that he hadn't been expecting such a call.

He wouldn't think about *her*. Or the night he'd spent in her arms. Or how cool and aloof she'd been ever since. Not that he could blame her. Hell, he and Hayes Daniels, his twin brother's CEO, had turned Mitchell into the feds the day after Jake had made love to her.

No doubt she was as guilty as her father. To think or feel anything about such a witch was a recipe for more disaster. No, the thing to do was to move on.

For a long moment he stared down at the miniature New Orleans he'd built. The structures, which were composed of cardboard, plastic and painted foam, looked vivid and exciting on his table against the window. When his icy-blue gaze swept to the model of the brazenly dramatic stadium that until five minutes ago he and his team had still dreamed of building, the hammer in his right temple pounded even more viciously.

Don't think about her.

Mitchell Butler had been rich and powerful and admired—until six weeks ago. Now his shipyard was bankrupt and his plans for a merger with Claiborne Energy defunct. His pampered daughter had been fired from her job as editor of the *Louisiana Observer*. Millions were missing from Butler's offshore bank in the Caymans and from Houses for Hurricane Victims. Or was it billions? The figures quoted by the media seemed to grow exponentially.

Mitchell was broke and so were his investors. Butler,

who was the most despised man in Louisiana, was responsible for ruining a lot of people besides Jake.

Tempted to smash the little buildings to the floor, Jake made a fist. He needed a few moments to himself to get his mind off the Butlers and regain his control.

Leaning against his desk and relaxing his hand, he stood there for a long moment, wondering how he'd tell his employees the bad news.

Better to face them now. Better to get it over with.

He jammed his hands into the pockets of his faded jeans and strode out of his private office into that of his secretary.

"Vanessa. Have everybody assemble in the boardroom. Say, in five minutes. And hold my calls."

Vanessa, who had twenty years on him and a will of iron hardened by a bitter marital experience, continued to tap steadily on her keyboard. She was a formidable worker, A single mother, she'd raised her three boys on her own.

Jake stepped closer to her desk and whispered, "It's not my fault your ex cheated on you and got that other woman pregnant."

Frowning, she pulled her gaze from her computer screen and looked up at him.

"Just checking to see if you even knew I was here or heard a word I said," he said.

"Five minutes. Boardroom. Everybody assemble. Hold calls." She poked her pencil into her bun, whirled, got on the intercom and barked out the order.

Ten minutes later, his headache much worse, Jake stood before sixty of his employees.

"I have some bad news," he said, stiffening when they whitened. He disliked disappointing those who counted on him almost as much as he hated failing.

"We can't get the funding we need to build the stadium. Jones won't even pay for our latest revisions to the designs…so I'm afraid I have no choice but to…"

He was about to mention he would be calling quite a few people into his office to discuss their termination when Vanessa whirled toward him looking as dark as those first ominous storm bands on the horizon that signaled a hurricane. She slapped a phone into his palm.

She was frowning so coldly he knew better than to ask what could possibly be more important than his informing his employees that because of Mitchell Butler he was going to have to let quite a few of them go.

"Your house alarm system went off. Your service says it's broken glass and that a perimeter has been breached."

"So? Tell them to send the police."

Vanessa's thin, painted eyebrows arched. "I did. Officer Thomas, who's on the phone, is there now. He says a Miss Alicia Butler's at your house demanding to see you and that she has her cat and a suitcase with her. What is this about?"

"I don't know."

But what was she doing there? She wouldn't return his calls and now she was at his house with her cat? Had she been trying to break in? Why? His pulse accelerated. With rage, he tried to tell himself.

"Claiborne speaking," he growled impatiently into the receiver.

"Mr. Claiborne. Officer Thomas. Sorry to bother you. You've got a yard full of reporters along with some angry hecklers."

"I know." They'd been there ever since a lead story in the newspaper had all but accused him of helping

Mitchell Butler embezzle funds from Houses for Hurricane Victims, a charity Jake had created and foolishly put Mitchell in charge of.

"A Miss Alicia Butler and her cat were on your veranda when I arrived, sir," the officer explained. "Apparently, some of her father's investors followed her from her apartment, and the crowd got pretty stirred up. Someone threw a brick through your front window and ran off. I've got Miss Butler and her cat in my patrol car. She's pretty shaken up, and her cat won't stop howling."

Although Jake rented his home, it was a large, modern house in a top-end neighborhood. Unfortunately, he lived next to his landlady, Jan Grant, who was both nosy and highly opinionated. Jan had already complained about rude reporters disrupting her mornings. The last thing he needed was for her to get upset about the arrival of the police and evict him.

"Officer, I'm sorry about all the excitement. Give me a minute. I was in the middle of something when you called."

Rubbing his brow, he tried to think what he should do. He wanted to deal with the layoffs now. But…Alicia, who'd been hounded in the papers and on television because of her father's problems, was in big trouble. She'd come to him for a reason. Why?

Ever since Mitchell had been federally indicted and put under house arrest, she'd been pestered by the federal government, the press and her father's investors. She'd looked thin and vulnerable in the pictures he'd seen of her on television.

Against his will he remembered a night that should never have happened and a delectable, silken, female body writhing beneath his…a body that had been in tune with his like no other. Prim and proper Alicia Butler had driven him past the brink of sanity. He wished he could erase all memories of her, but despite what he'd learned about her father since that evening, he hadn't been able to.

Indeed, he'd thought about Alicia and how sweet she'd seemed and what they had done that night too often. Hell, they'd barely managed to get inside his house and lock his door before they'd stripped and made love.

Aware that his employees were watching him and hanging on his every word, he realized he had to get his mind off sex with Alicia and act quickly.

"You said she has her cat with her? And a suitcase?"

Alarm bells that had more to do with memories of Alicia's sensuality than her cat and suitcase had his temple throbbing harder than ever.

She hadn't come to see him on a whim.

"The girl seems unwell."

"Whatever…do you mean?" Jake asked, suddenly more concerned than he should have been.

"Her voice is so soft I can barely hear her."

Jake's eyes burned as he remembered the honeyed tones of Alicia's cultured voice whispering his name as he'd made love to her. Why did every detail about their night together stand out?

The faces of his employees blurred.

"I'll come home immediately and take care of this," he said.

Sounding relieved, the officer said a quick goodbye.

Jake handed the phone to Vanessa.

"I didn't realize you were personally involved with

Alicia Butler," Vanessa hissed as soon as she had him all to herself in his office.

Her accusing tone set him on edge. The last thing he desired was the third degree from his secretary. Without looking at her, he grabbed his keys out of a drawer and slung his jacket over one shoulder.

"I'm not," he lied.

"Then what is she doing on your doorstep?"

"I can't let you know until I find out, now, can I?"

"I don't like the sound of this. If there are reporters and cops along with Alicia at your house, there'll be more bad publicity. The Butlers are thieves. You'll be tarred with the same brush. We're barely surviving this downturn as it is."

"You think I don't know that? I'm already taking the rap for what Mitchell did. Look, why don't you concentrate on taking care of things here while I go to see what she wants, okay?"

"You're right, of course. This whole thing just has me upset."

When he reached the parking garage, his gut twisted as he thought about all the people he'd have to fire later because of Alicia Butler and her father.

Damn her.

When Jake braked sharply in his drive, six reporters stampeded across the wet grass toward him. There had been only one this morning. No sooner did he open his door than they shoved raised microphones at his face.

The curtain next door on Jan Grant's front window was pulled aside and he made out the stout bulk of his landlady, who wasn't about to miss anything.

A snicker from the closest reporter. "What was Alicia Butler doing on your doorstep?"

Instead of dignifying the man with an answer, Jake focused on the slim figure hunched in the back of the single patrol car parked in front of his home beyond the reporters' dripping black umbrellas. Then he looked at the broken window beside his front door.

He knew he should hate Alicia, but he couldn't forget the beating she'd taken from the press for the past few weeks. Ever since that article about how he'd appointed Mitchell Butler treasurer of Houses for Hurricane Victims, and about how all the funds had vanished, he'd really been able to relate to what she must have been going through.

She looked too crushed and defenseless cowering in the back of that car, so utterly unlike the tall, elegant woman he'd bedded or the defiant woman who'd told him to go to hell the next morning. He couldn't hate her. Fool that he was, his chest constricted with sympathy.

A cop, who was probably Officer Thomas, pointed needlessly toward his car. "She's over there."

"Thanks."

Jake loped past the reporters, his Italian loafers sinking into the ooze of his soaked lawn as he made his way toward the patrol car.

"Alicia?" he muttered in a harsh tone as he rapped his knuckles on the glass window.

She rolled the window down a few inches and his gaze roved the length of her willowy body, taking in her white, translucent skin. Mascara ran beneath her long-lashed, almond-shaped, brown eyes. Wet, dark ropes of her hair stuck to her neck. Despite her thinness and her pallor, she affected him every bit as intensely as she had their one night together.

Opening the door, he took her hand, which felt icy, and helped her out.

She wore a white, gauzy dress that clung. When his gaze lingered on the raindrops moistening her full lips, he remembered with an almost visceral ache exactly how soft that mouth had been against his and exactly how sweet she'd tasted.

His lips thinned as other memories of the intimacies they'd shared assaulted him. With all her problems, why was she here?

"Thank you for coming so fast," she said.

"How did you get here?" he asked.

"Taxi."

"Well, you were reckless to come in a public taxi and let your horde follow you."

"I—I didn't think. Sorry I embarrassed you."

"You could have called me. We could have met somewhere discreet."

"Sorry. I hate all this as much as you do."

The officer had been right about her looking ill. The brown eyes that had sparkled with fire each and every time he'd kissed her or licked her *that* night were dull and glazed with pain.

"Meow!"

Frowning, Jake looked across his yard and saw Officer Thomas talking to the reporters. Jake's selfish agenda would be best served if he told the officer to see about her. But an unhealthy mixture of curiosity, sympathy and some self-destructive emotion that was better left unanalyzed overpowered him.

Fool that he was, instead of signaling for the policeman, he grabbed her hand and pointed her in the direction of the sidewalk that led to his front door. Then he leaned inside the car and picked up Alicia's suitcase and her cat carrier. Hissing, the animal lunged at the walls of his cage. Ignoring the beast, Jake strode up the walk after Alicia. Pulling out his keys, he unlocked his door, then thrust it open so violently it banged the wood paneling of his interior wall.

He stood to one side so that she could enter. Reluctant to follow him, she remained frozen, her skirt dripping, her eyes staring at him, so he said, "In case you didn't notice, I'm inviting you inside."

"I noticed," she whispered in a sexy croak that unnerved him.

"So, ladies first."

A bolt of lightning was followed by a crash of thunder. Then several flashbulbs went off in their faces.

Yowling, Gus hurled himself against the side of the cage, rocking it even harder.

"Your cat says he thinks going inside would be a very good idea," Jake said.

"He has issues about water, not to mention thunder."

"Well, if you came over here to grant interviews on my porch, enjoy. But Gus and I have had enough of our five minutes of fame. We'd prefer to go inside and open a can of tuna."

Once he had set her cat and her bag down inside his ultramodern foyer, which was now covered in glass shards, he ran his hand along the slick, polished surface of his paneled wall until he found the light switch. Flipping it on, he looked back outside. She was still glaring at him.

"Your foyer is not exactly neutral territory," she whispered.

"Don't remind me."

Suddenly he was remembering how they'd torn off their clothes the last time they'd stepped across his threshold. He hadn't bothered to turn on any lights. Once

naked, they'd launched themselves at each other. Heat
engulfed him as he remembered how they'd sunk to the
floor, and he'd straddled her on top of the Kilim carpet
on which he now stood. He'd thought her adorable and
sexy as hell.

More flashbulbs captured her ashen face.

The worried little crease between her dark brows
deepened and she went even whiter. When he reached
for her anxiously, she sprang away from him and jumped
across the threshold.

Damn it, he'd only wanted to soothe her. Hell, maybe
it was a good thing she'd stopped him.

She plastered herself against his mahogany wall as
far away from him as possible, her delectable breasts
heaving beneath that thin white dress that clung
closely.

The memory of what he'd done to those pink-tipped
breasts made him feel much too warm. With a start he
realized he'd awakened every night since aching for her
sweetness and sexiness.

Annoyed that she was so afraid of him and he so
jittery around her, Jake slammed his door. Once it
was bolted against the goggle-eyed reporters and their
flashbulbs, she began to shiver.

"You're freezing," he said, stating the obvious in a
harsh tone to conceal his concern.

"S-sorry. A-air-c-conditioning." Struggling for control, she sucked in a breath. "I'm dripping all over your
fancy floor, too."

"It's stone. It won't melt. But wait here. I'll turn the
AC off and get you some towels."

Thankful for an excuse to leave her and get a grip on
himself, he strode down the hall before she could object
and quickly adjusted the thermostat. Ducking into his

guest bath, he grabbed some fluffy white towels. When he returned, he ripped off his jacket and wrapped it around her shoulders and placed the thick towels in her hands.

Although their fingers touched briefly, it was long enough for him to register that her soft skin felt like ice.

With a breathless sound she cringed away from him.

"Thank you," she whispered as she wrapped a towel around her head and began to pat her hair dry. "I'm s-sorry to be so much trouble."

"No trouble." He tore his gaze from her stricken face.

How could he actually want to help her? Whatever was wrong was no business of his. There were at least a dozen reasons why he should hate her, most of them names of people his charity couldn't build houses for and employees he would soon be forced to fire. But she looked too much like a drowned waif for him to even consider chastising her in any way at this point. The feds and reporters hounding her seemed to have that job well in hand.

Steeling himself against the impulse to hold her close until his body warmth made her stop shaking, his voice was rougher when he spoke. "You'll feel better when we get you out of those wet clothes and dry you off."

"We?" She blushed at his suggestion. His own heart began to thud as he realized how that comment had sounded. With an effort he forced himself to look anywhere but at her softly alluring breasts.

Had she deliberately dressed in that filmy, see-through number so he'd want to stare at them? Impotent rage that she could arouse him so easily swept over him.

"What I meant to say is there's a bathroom down the hall. You probably remember showering in it."

When she reddened, he wished he hadn't reminded them both they'd showered together.

"I'll bring you a robe and more fresh towels," he said, his tone more clipped.

Glad for the excuse to leave her again, he went back down the hall. But he was soon much too aware of her heels clicking rapidly on the flagstones behind him.

When she stepped inside the bath, the beige marble walls seemed to close in, trapping him. Staring down at her, he recalled again how they'd laughingly showered after making love all over his house. He'd washed her hair, dried her off, taken her back to bed where he'd held her close for hours.

He backed out of the bathroom on the pretense of finding her more towels and his robe. For his own sanity he knew he should figure out what she wanted and then get rid of her as soon as possible. But as he grabbed the robe off a hook in his master bath, he knew he wasn't going to do anything so sensible.

She'd fascinated him from the first moment he'd seen her in that tight gold sheath on his brother's arm at his grandfather's eightieth birthday party. When Cici had asked him to look after Alicia so she could dance with Logan, he'd jumped at the chance. Then Logan had disappeared with Cici, and he'd offered to drive the stranded Alicia home.

Over a late-night coffee he'd found her even sweeter than she was gorgeous—not at all like her calculating father. A writer and an editor, she hadn't been the shallow rich girl he'd expected. She'd been intelligent and insightful. When he'd kissed her after she'd laughed at one of his jokes, they'd both gone up in flames.

The morning after they'd made love, Logan's CEO, Hayes Daniels, had presented him with irrefutable proof that her father was a criminal. When Jake and his CPA had checked the books and bank statements for Houses for Hurricane Victims, they'd discovered alarming discrepancies. Jake had gone with Hayes to turn Mitchell in to the feds.

Since her father was a crook, a crook he'd blown the whistle on, Jake should rid himself of her immediately. But she looked so lost.

Even after he'd discovered her father had robbed Houses for Hurricane Victims, she'd consumed his thoughts. He'd called her repeatedly. Not that she'd answered. No doubt she blamed him for her father's downfall.

How could he still find her attractive? But he did.

From their first tentative kiss, when her velvet-tipped fingers had singed his flesh through his cotton shirt and her lips had been so soft and hot as they'd parted for his tongue, his groin had tightened with unbearable need.

That a single kiss could have given such a contagion of pleasure should have been a warning. Instead, he'd staked his claim by arching her body against his.

He still wanted her. Which meant he should make her leave before he did something really stupid.

Two

After sweeping up the glass in the foyer and opening a can of tuna in the kitchen, Jake was unlocking the cat crate to let the beast out when he heard a crash from the bathroom.

Ears flat, the cat raced out of the kitchen so fast he collided with a china flowerpot and knocked it over.

Ignoring the cat and the dirt spilling from the shattered pot, Jake ran down the hall to check on Alicia.

"Alicia?"

When she didn't answer, panic slammed him.

"Alicia? Alicia! Are you all right?"

No answer.

When he pounded on the door with his fists and there was no response, he tried the doorknob, which turned. He shoved it and the door flew open, thick vapors enveloping him. "Alicia?"

Blindly he made his way through the steamy mists to the glassed-in shower-tub and slid the door open.

Through the steam he saw her lying in a crumpled heap, warm water streaming over her naked thighs. Shutting off the faucet, he leaned down and picked her up. Grabbing the towels and robe she'd placed on a stool, he clutched the unconscious woman and carried her down the hall into his den. She wasn't heavy, so he bore her easily.

He was careful not to a glance at her nude body more than necessary. Still, his gaze did linger on the heart-shaped birthmark on her left breast that he'd once tongued so ardently the night he'd made love to her. Settling her onto his couch, he couldn't have cared less how the water might stain the expensive leather. He was too worried about her.

He lifted her wrist and felt a pulse. He smiled when it was steady and strong. Maybe she'd knelt down for something she'd dropped and had stood up too fast.

"Alicia! Wake up!"

She mumbled something he didn't understand and then turned her face away from him.

Had she hit her head? Did she have a concussion?

"Daddy!" she whispered. "Daddy! Where are you? Why can't you ever, just this once, stay home?"

Was she delirious? Thinking to inspect her scalp for injuries, Jake slid his fingers through her hair. Parting the thick waves with his blunt fingers, he discovered a lump.

"Open your eyes!" he commanded.

Much to his surprise, the long, feminine lashes fluttered. Her plump, sexy lips quivered.

Brown irises slowly filled with light as she struggled

to focus. "Jake…it's you? What's wrong? Why are you shouting at me?"

She reached out and took his big hand, sending a sexual shock of awareness through him. "Where am I?"

"My living room."

"What am I doing here?"

That was the question upper most on his mind, but he couldn't ask her until he was sure she was all right.

Slowly, as she continued to stare at him, her expression changed.

"Where are my clothes?" Her voice rose. "What did you to me?"

"Not a damn thing that I shouldn't have, so calm down. You fell in the shower. I heard a crash, rushed inside, turned the water off, carried you here, dried you, put you into my robe and checked your pulse. And now that you're conscious and yourself again, I think we should call your doctor."

"No need for that! I'm fine," she said huffily. "Or at least I would be if…" She stopped, clearly troubled by some new thought.

"Did you faint? Or trip?"

She stared at him. Her eyes were huge, wary. "Everything just went black. I guess I fainted."

"Like I said, you should see a doctor."

"I will. But not right now. I'm very hungry. I…I haven't eaten much for a couple of days."

He'd read in some newspaper that reporters stalked her every time she left her apartment, even to go to the grocery store. Had she been starving herself as a result? Again, he fought the impulse to feel sorry for her.

"Could I possibly trouble you for a cracker…or two…

and maybe some tea?" she asked, her tone formal and polite now.

She and her father had made a mess of his life. He should forget she looked defenseless and sexy and make himself call the cops and ask them to send Officer Thomas back. Jake could ask him to drive her to a soup kitchen or a hospital—anywhere.

This whole thing was beginning to feel much too complicated. But instead of doing anything remotely sensible, he nodded.

"Why did you come here?" he demanded.

She rubbed the back of her head and winced. "Jake, before we get into that, I—I'm, I really am seeing bright spots. I...I...I really do need that cracker first."

"You threatening to faint on me again?"

"I don't feel so good. Really, I don't. That's a fact... not a threat."

"One stale cracker coming right up," he whispered gently. "You stay put on the couch while I make a tray. The last thing either of us need is for you to faint again."

As Jake's footsteps receded, Alicia sat up on his couch and squeezed her eyes shut.

Oh, God, how could she tell him, him of all people, the man who'd turned her father in to the feds and blown his life and her to bits, that she might be pregnant with his baby?

She'd tested positive on four home pregnancy tests. *Four.*

Pressing her fingers to her temple, she counted her thudding heartbeats until the bright spots faded.

It wasn't as if she hadn't rehearsed a little speech— several speeches.

*Jake, every morning I wake up clammy with nausea.
Just for the record, my period's three weeks late…. I
know that because I always note the event by writing a
little p—in red—on my kitchen calendar on the exact
date of the month. And I'm never late!*

She knew what he'd say—that it wasn't possible, that
he'd used a condom. Several condoms.

She sucked in a tight breath as too many embar-
rassingly intimate memories flickered. Sex had never
been her favorite sport. She was too shy and repressed.
Sex was something a woman like her never even
considered with a virtual stranger. But she'd forgotten
all her aversions and hang-ups with Jake. She'd given
herself to him, a man she'd barely known, with such
uncharacteristic abandon she blushed every time she
thought about how many times and where they'd done
it.

And then the next morning he and Hayes Daniels had
turned her father in to the feds. Shivering, she must have
sat there on his couch twisting that strand of hair for a
full five minutes. Even in his thick robe, she felt chilled
to the bone. Well, at least the awful morning sickness
had passed.

He'd think she was crazy for not waiting to tell him
until she was sure. But—because of him—she hadn't
had a choice. The feds, or rather that officious little agent
with the wire-rimmed glasses atop his bulbous nose,
had shown up without warning and had kicked her out
of her apartment, explaining again why the feds had the
right to seize all her father's properties, which included
her apartment and furniture.

She wouldn't have come here if she'd had anywhere
else to go. Before she'd left the apartment, she'd tried her
father's cell phone. He had caller ID, so if his phone was

near, he'd know she was calling. But he hadn't answered. Had he seen her name and punched the word *ignore?*

Sometimes she thought that that little button on his phone was a metaphor for the way he'd always treated her. Everything else in his life had always come before her. Jake, on the other hand, had come home as soon as he'd known she was here. Not that she liked him… or anything; not after what he'd done. Still, he'd shown up the minute he'd heard she was in trouble. And he'd invited her inside.

Clutching his robe and knotting the sash tightly, Alicia rose and tiptoed down the hall to his kitchen. One foot into the kitchen, she stiffened at the sight of the kitchen table where Jake had made love to her so heatedly he'd sent silverware and plates crashing to the floor.

Desperate to shift her attention away from the embarrassing memory that had her pulse thudding she stared at Gus's empty carrier, which lay on its side. Broken bits of a pot she vaguely remembered having admired in the hall earlier littered the counter.

"Where's poor Gus?"

"Poor Gus, my eye. When I let him out of his carrier, he practically tore the place apart. Broke a pot that doesn't belong to me."

"You better not have hurt him."

"He made a clean break. I was too worried about you to chase him."

"Oh."

"I cut some cheese and peeled a banana to go along with the apple that I also peeled for you. Sorry to disappoint, but I don't have any stale crackers."

She bit her lip to keep from grinning.

Watching her guardedly, he set a plate on the table.

She grabbed a piece of apple and began to munch noisily as she admired his handiwork. He'd done rather a good job with the food actually.

Some of her anxiety drained away. It was suddenly too easy to remember why she'd fallen for Jake that night and gotten herself into this mess. Her father had confided to her that he was in terrible trouble, so she'd been worried even before Logan had disappeared with Cici at the party.

Then Jake had appeared, insisting he'd take care of her. He'd been so warm and attentive, and soon they'd been able to talk about anything. In no time she'd found herself having fun just drinking coffee with him and laughing at his stories about his adventures in the wild. Unfortunately, she'd confided her concerns about her father.

Jake place a fork, knife and napkin on the table and sat down across from her. His chocolate-dark hair fell across his brow and temple. He was so close, and he looked so sexy as he watched too intently.

She set her apple sliver down and avoided his gaze. But his having taken trouble with the plate pleased her—too much. Why did she always read more into small kindnesses than she should?

It was a plate of food, that was all. He'd fed Gus, hadn't he? He didn't like Gus, did he?

"Eat," Jake said gently. "A single bite won't do you much good."

She thought about the baby that they might be having together and blushed. How to tell him?

"How can I, with you watching me?"

No sooner did he stand up than his phone rang.

"Sorry," he said. "It's my secretary. I left things in a mess. I'd better take this."

He stepped into the hall and pulled the door shut.

After that Alicia could only catch bits and pieces of his conversation.

"Yes, I'm coming back—

"How can you think I could have forgotten them—

"No, she hasn't told me why, not that this is any of your business—

"Damn it. That's what I'm trying to determine—

"Pregnant? I suggest you get your mind out of the gutter and focus on your work instead of my personal affairs—which, by the way, are none of your business…."

Pregnant.

The woman was an oracle.

Her appetite gone in the space of a heartbeat, Alicia knew she had to tell him the truth, and fast.

Thankfully, he was much too annoyed at his secretary to even glance at her as he strode back in.

"You've barely touched your food. Why?" he demanded, his voice colder as he set his phone down.

"Bad news, huh?"

"I have a life. Not that you probably give a damn what I was doing before the cops called me about you."

"Try me."

"I was just about to fire a lot of hardworking people, people who really need their jobs."

"And your secretary thinks it's all my fault."

So many people blamed her for what her father had supposedly done. Some believed he'd stashed a fortune in a secret, offshore account in her name.

Her father said he was innocent and she wanted to believe him. Not that it was easy when everybody else thought he was guilty. And what did it matter whether he was innocent or not when her own bank accounts here in New Orleans and her credit cards were frozen? When two days ago Sam, her editor in chief, had caved in to mounting pressure to fire her from the editorial/writer job that she'd dearly loved. She had no money, no job, no reputation and no future. And four home pregnancy tests had been positive.

His anger crackled between them. "People distrust me now. Whatever I think about who's to blame, I need to get back to the office. So, what do you say we cut to the chase? Why are you here?"

"You have an incredibly smart secretary."

"What the hell does she have to do with anything?"

"I think I'm pregnant."

He looked so dumbstruck, she truly felt sorry for him.

"What? No way!"

Three

His legs spread apart, Jake towered over Alicia as she silently hunched lower at his kitchen table. "Would you kindly repeat that."

"You heard me."

"Did you say you think…you're pregnant. You don't know? Why would you come here before you were sure?"

His glowering made her squirm uneasily. "I took four pregnancy tests, and they were all positive. I can't eat. And I fainted, didn't I? I've been nauseated the last two mornings. My period's late. I could go on with the symptoms. Did I tell you I really like pickles right now? What do you think all that adds up to?"

A sledgehammer was pounding in his brain.

"Plus, because of you the feds kicked me out of my apartment, and I have nowhere to stay."

"Have you had your condition confirmed by a doctor?" he asked.

She grabbed another sliver of apple. Shaking her head, she bit into it. "Not yet, but the way things have been going, I'd bet my miserable life that we're probably pregnant."

"We…"

"We!"

"Okay, but you could still be wrong about…*us*." He looked sick to be using the plural pronoun.

"Right…. Four pregnancy tests can definitely be wrong on planet Earth. Anything in our magical realm is possible," she said dully.

"Could be a bad batch."

Shaking her head at him, she decided to try the white cheese he'd put out. In between bouts of nausea, she had a voracious appetite. What she really wanted was a dill pickle. Not that she was about to ask for one.

His face was hard and set as he watched her. "And you're sure that if you are…"

Beneath his critical gaze, she lost her craving as a strange panic welled up inside her. She'd told him she couldn't eat with him staring at her like that, but his mood was so bitter she thought maybe now wasn't a good time to nag, so she laid the piece of cheese back on the platter.

"What? What is it? Why are you scowling at me like that?" she said. "What have I done now?"

He took a deep, worried breath.

"What?" she demanded.

"Sorry I have to ask this. Are you absolutely sure that…if you're right…about *you* being pregnant…that I'm…that I'm the father?"

Vertigo made his granite countertops whirl round and round. His darkly handsome face blurred sickeningly.

"You moralistic jerk!" Fury consuming her, she sprang out of the chair and lunged at him. "Am I sure? Damn right I'm sure!"

He caught her wrist in midair and used it to swing her against the long length of his muscular body. Her full breasts slid against his ripped torso. In an effort to catch herself, she grabbed his lean waist. Then she fought to launch herself free of him. He used the leverage to pull her closer.

"Calm down. I just had to be sure."

"I'm totally positive," she yelled, kicking at him even as she pushed at his chest. "I told you that you're the only man I've….I've slept with…in months."

His eyes had taken on the polar chill of blue ice chips. "What about my brother?"

Fury suffused her.

"Your father said you were going to marry him," Jake persisted.

"My father made that up. Logan and I dated, but our relationship didn't work on any level other than friendship. Not that my lack of a sex life is any of your business!"

"Maybe I disagree. After all, you claim I'm the father of your child."

"If I'm pregnant, so are you! Not that I would choose you!"

"Nor I you!"

"Believe me, I…I wish it was somebody else's! Somebody I met in a bar would be nicer! So let me go!"

"Are you going to try to hit me again if I do?"

"After what you just said, you deserve a bullet…you know where. But no, since I'm a lady."

"You could have fooled me." Releasing her, he watched her warily.

She backed a few steps away from him and rubbed her wrist.

"Okay," he said. "I'm sorry to upset you, but I had to know. I used condoms, if you'll remember. Lots of them. I took precautions."

"Oh, yeah, well, you didn't take enough!"

He stared at her for a long moment. "I'm sorry," he repeated. "If what you say is true, and you're pregnant, and it's mine, I'll accept full responsibility for the child…and for you…despite who you are…which means our next step should be to see a doctor."

"If what I say is true? *If?* You still don't believe me?" Her eyes narrowed and her pulse sped up. "Well, it's true! *Despite who you are!* I hate this…."

"So the hell do I, but it looks like we're stuck with each other, at least until we get some sound medical advice."

"I'm afraid a doctor will only confirm the worst!"

"Obviously, you believe that," he said. "But I won't believe it until I hear him say it."

"Dr. Preston's a she. When she does, then what?"

"We'll handle it," he muttered.

"Well, if you think you can make me stop this pregnancy…"

His black brows slashed together. It was his turn to hiss in a breath and gape at her. "You don't know me at all if you think I'd destroy my child."

His outrage was so intense, she knotted her hands and stood up taller.

"How could I know what you feel on the subject or

on any subject, when for all practical purposes we're strangers?" she whispered.

"Strangers, *cher?* You wish. I wish. Unfortunately, that's the last thing we are. I'd say we're intimately connected."

"I shouldn't have come. Look, I'll figure out how to do this on my own. I have a friend in London who's offered... Never mind! Forget I ever came here."

"As if I could."

She turned away from him and stared at his backyard, which looked overgrown and badly in need of pruning. She did so love working with plants. Oh, how could she think of gardening at a time like this?

Jake was silent and still for a long moment, but she imagined his eyes boring into her back. Then his breath sped up, and he spanned the distance that separated them.

"I don't want you to go," he said, planting his hands on her shoulders. "You were right to come here. We'll figure this out...together."

Before she knew what he was about, he'd pulled her tightly against him. Some part of her wanted to twist out of his grasp, but another wanted to relax into his hard warmth and strength, so she let him pull her closer. The times when someone had held her and comforted her in life had been so rare since her mother's death, and that night with him had been wonderful.

Then the next day her father's empire had crashed very publicly, and her father had told her that Jake had been one of the main whistle-blowers who'd brought him down.

"I am to blame for what happened that night," Jake muttered against her throat, his voice deepening with needs that at first she did not understand. "I wanted you and you wanted me, too. I didn't realize what your father had done until the next day."

"No."

She shut her eyes, but it was impossible to ignore how wonderful she felt in his arms. Only gradually did she grow aware that he had become aroused.

"Stop this!" she whispered, trying to pull away.

"God help me, I still want you," he whispered, snugging her even closer. "You feel the same. Kiss me."

His husky tone and his hot, male body molded so tightly against her with such ardent need triggered... something.

She knew she should fight him, but instead she twisted around, ever so slightly, just enough so that she could tilt her mouth up to his.

He claimed her lips, hesitantly at first, but soon took all she was willing to give as greedily as he had the night he'd made love to her. He kissed her long and hard, his tongue plunging between her lips. She gasped as an answering desire began to course through her blood.

The sash of his robe came loose, and he yanked the edges of the robe aside, cupping her breasts, tracing his thumbs across her nipples, which were tight and hard. Ripping his shirt out of his slacks, he pulled it up, so that when he dragged her even closer, her breasts were mashed against his bare chest.

Contact with the coarse hair of his torso made her nipples peak and her blood burn.

"Oh, no." She felt crazy with unwanted needs. Against her will, she arched her body so that her legs and thighs fitted his. His skin grew so hot she felt as if she was being consumed in a roaring furnace.

He was right about her wanting him. Limp with

desire, she felt meltingly alive caught in his hard, strong arms. His mouth was on hers again and it was as if their bodies spoke a language all their own. Everything about him was sensually delicious and made her feel starved for more.

Despite his part in bringing her father down, she'd remembered his kisses and lovemaking longingly, and every night she'd dreamed of him and had awakened in the dead of the night, her body aching for his mouth and hands to caress her like this again, even though she denied it.

"I want you," he said softly. "Despite everything, I want you on my kitchen table. On my foyer floor. In my bed. On my couch. In my shower. I want to repeat everything we did before. I want to do it again and again and more…until I'm too weak to stand and you have to feed me by hand in bed to revive me. And when I do revive, I'll want you all over again."

"God help me, I want all that, too," she admitted shakily.

In that moment she actually believed she would never want to die anywhere else but in his arms.

Then he kissed her again, nibbling her lower lip at first. Gradually his kiss lengthened and grew hard. He fused his mouth to hers endlessly, his tongue mating with hers until she felt she was burning up like a star. She could hardly breathe when he pulled away at last.

"You are beautiful," he said gently. "Unforgettable." His hand slid over her body until his fingers closed over her plump breast. "Easy to talk to. And fun. I've thought about these breasts, their softness and the tightness of your nipples many many times these past few weeks. In fact I couldn't stop thinking about you or them, no matter how diligently I tried."

"Which means you don't really like me…if you don't even want to think about me," she said, struggling to regain her senses. "All you feel is lust."

Part of her wished he'd deny it.

"Call it whatever you like, it's very powerful," he said.

"Let me go," she whispered. "Please…. This will only make an impossible situation worse."

"But I want you," he insisted.

"We have more serious things to think about. Plans to make. We're already in over our heads as it is."

"Have you ever had a habit you couldn't break?"

"Is that what I am to you—a bad habit?"

Pulling her closer even as she fought to resist him again, he gripped her arms hard. But just as he brought his mouth down to hers and she thought she would soon be lost on a wild, dark tide, he froze.

For a long moment he stood as immobile as a statue. He stared down at her as if he were struggling as hard as she was for control. Then he cursed low under his breath and pushed free of her.

Feeling hurt and rejected, which made zero sense, she jerked the edges of the robe together and spun away.

Hot color flared in his cheeks, too; a savage muscle was jumping along his jawline. His devouring gaze flamed with a fierce blue light.

"Sorry," he finally muttered in an edgy, unapologetic tone. Then he rubbed his jaw where the muscle twitched. "I don't know what…happened. I…I just lost control there for a second. Sorry."

He looked down at the floor and raked a hand through his mussed dark hair. Then he clumsily jammed the edges of his shirt into his waistband. "If I can't trust myself around you, even knowing what you are, I've got to get the hell out of here."

One minute he'd been out to prove she desired him; in the next he was running as scared as she was. And all because he'd lost his precious control.

She clenched her teeth and then unclenched them. "But we have to decide what to do."

He took a deep breath. "First we have to find out if we have a problem or not. You need to call your doctor, make an appointment as fast as possible."

"I need a place to stay tonight. Because of you, the feds took my apartment, all my furniture…and my car. I have no friends left in Louisiana." She paused. When he didn't say no immediately, she said, "I'd need a litter box and litter for Gus."

"Okay. Of course, you can stay here if you like. But if you do, I'm moving out."

"Where?"

"I don't know."

"You mean I'll be here alone?"

"Just for tonight. Trust me. You're better off with me gone. I don't know what just happened between us or why. But I'll be fine once I get off to myself, do some thinking and get a grip. I don't like feeling trapped in this situation with you."

"And you think I like it?"

"I'm not a mind reader, so I can only take your word for how you feel."

She envied the way he could compartmentalize, the way his deep voice sounded almost cool and contained now when her heart was still racing.

Trying to copy him, she took a deep breath and tried to push down her emotions. It was probably better that they spend the night apart.

"Okay then," she said. "Sounds like a plan."

"I'll give you my cell number. Call me after you make that appointment with your doctor." He pulled a set of car keys out of his pocket. "I want to know when and where it is."

"You're leaving now?"

"I've got to get back to my office. Like I told you before—because of you, *cher,* I've got a lot of nice people to fire."

"I'm sorry about that." She truly was.

He hesitated. "Just so you know where I'll be... Tonight I think I'll drive out to Belle Rose and spend the night in a friend's houseboat in the swamp. I need to be by myself—to think."

She arched her brows. Poor guy. If it hadn't been for his part in her father's downfall, she might have felt sorry for him.

He'd been having a bad day even before she'd showed up on his doorstep and announced they might be pregnant. And what had he done—he'd given up his house for the night, so she'd have a safe place to stay.

Four

When the sagging roofline of Bos's houseboat loomed out of the steamy gloom of shadowy dwarf palmettos, bald cypress trees and water tupelo, Jake cut the motor and sprang toward the bow. He'd hoped he'd experience at least a slight lifting of his mood once he was out of the city and had returned to his boyhood refuge. Despite the familiar roar of bull alligators, locusts and frogs, he felt like a stranger in a foreign land. His leaden heart kept him alienated from all that should have been familiar and dear.

Images of a big-eyed, pale Alicia in the patrol car, the dull stares of his employees after he'd let them go, Cici's and Logan's radiant smiles at their wedding bombarded him in a never-ending loop. The thick heat of the swamp pressed too close, making him feel trapped by business and personal problems—and most of it was the Butlers' fault.

The air was dank with the stench of rot and mold. He would have preferred to be rock climbing in Utah or Alaska rather than hanging out in the swamp. Still, this was the wild and life was always simpler in the wild. He kept a cabin south of Denali National Park in Alaska that he visited every summer. Too bad he didn't have time to go there now. It was the one place that was far enough away from his real life so that he could count on solitude there clearing his mind.

Grabbing the bowline, he spread his legs so that he stood in the middle of the eight-foot aluminum flatboat as it drifted silently through the mirror-black swamp water toward the houseboat.

A night to himself even in this wild place wasn't long enough to sort it all out, but it was a start. If Alicia was pregnant, he couldn't abandon his kid—even if she was Mitchell Butler's daughter.

He thought about the families still living in three-room trailers to whom he'd promised homes before the funds to build them had vanished—because of her father.

Wrapping the line around a rusting cleat, Jake made sure the flatboat was snug against the used tires Bos had nailed as crude fenders along the side of the houseboat. Then he ran his gaze over the shabby structure.

The houseboat had two tiny bedrooms, a kitchen, no bath. Surprisingly, the place didn't look any worse for wear. It must've been a good ten years since he was last here. Bos had been ill of late, but when Jake had visited him a month ago, he'd told him he'd managed to do what was necessary to maintain it.

"Not that I get out to the houseboat much these days," Bos had said. "You're welcome to it—just like always, anytime. The fishin's still pretty good even if the water in the swamp gets saltier every year."

Bos was another man who felt the need to get away from civilization upon occasion.

With a frown Jake set his gear down beside Bos's stacked crab traps. After opening the door to the cabin, he pitched his backpack inside.

This fish camp was located between the Claibornes' ancestral mansion, Belle Rose, and Bos's less developed properties to the south of Belle Rose. Pierre, Jake's grandfather, had never approved of Jake hanging out at Bos's camp in the swamp when Jake had been a kid. The truth was, his grandfather had detested Bos with an irrational passion. The old man had considered Bos, who'd run a bar and fought cocks, a bad influence, so most of the time Jake had chosen to sneak off, willingly risking the consequences of Grand-père's rage later.

A rebel from birth, Jake had been as fascinated by Bos's bad reputation as his grandfather had been repelled by it. Not that Bos was really such a bad sort once you got to know him. Bos had adopted his orphaned niece Cici, hadn't he? He'd understood what it was like not to feel you fit into your family, and he'd taken Jake hunting and fishing and crabbing without even so much as asking a single prying question about his need to escape his domineering grandfather and cocky older twin.

Bos had encouraged him to learn to fend for himself in the wild, so as soon as he'd been old enough, Jake had explored the endless marshes and bayous on his own, hunting doves and ducks and swimming off forested islands.

Back then Noonoon, his nanny, used to fuss at him, saying she couldn't keep a glass jar in the house because

Jake was always borrowing them to house his crabs and frogs and minnows and turtles.

Jake smiled briefly at the memory of Noonoon's dark face until concern about Alicia alone in his house intruded.

She was fine, he told himself. She was a big girl. He'd showed her how to set the alarm. Hell, he'd even sent Vanessa over to his house to make sure Alicia had everything she needed.

Alicia was fine.

Why couldn't he forget how pale and shaken she'd looked in that patrol car?

His stomach growled, reminding him that he hadn't brought any groceries.

Forget her.

He was hungry. If he was going to eat, he had to shoot something or catch something.

Whatever she'd expected when she'd come to Jake's house, it wasn't kindness and concern.

"If you don't need anything else, I really do have to get home to my boys." Vanessa's voice was crisp and hurried and yet there was a maternal compassion in her dark brown eyes that reminded Alicia of her own mother.

Alicia caught herself. This woman was a stranger. She had a life and didn't have much time to deal even briefly with her boss's personal crisis. Mothering her sons was her top priority.

"I'll be fine," Alicia whispered. "Thanks for sending that man over to board up the window."

"You could spend the night with me and my boys if you're afraid to stay in such a big house all by yourself."

"What a sweet offer, but really, I'll be fine," Alicia said. "It's just the night."

"I'd enjoy some adult companionship," Vanessa coaxed.

Alicia shook her head.

"Okay, then. He told me to tell you to set the alarm. And if you get lonely—call."

Nodding at the older woman, who Jake had paid to take care of her, Alicia held on to the two sacks of groceries as Vanessa shut the front door and then locked it firmly behind her.

Clutching the grocery sacks to her breasts, Alicia walked back to the kitchen. Mechanically she removed the lunch meat and cereal boxes, a loaf of bread and a bottle of milk and set them on the counter. It was nice of Jake to send food.

The last rays of the setting sun gilded the edges between the shades and the windowsill. Soon it would be dark outside. She had the rest of the evening to think about her problem. At least Jake had listened and said he would assume his share of the responsibility. He hadn't thrown her out.

She wished he was here, and that confused her. She'd felt so wonderful when he'd held her and kissed her. That perplexed her, too. How could she feel this powerful connection to a man who'd made love to her and then had turned her father in to the feds?

Maybe it was being in this house, where they'd talked and laughed and made love. They had so much fun together that first night.

Don't think about it!

Okay, enough! I have things to do. I'll make supper, clean the dishes, get ready for bed, hunt for Gus, watch some TV, set my alarm.

Is it really so important to set an alarm when my doctor's appointment tomorrow isn't until noon?

Just do it.

She called to Gus, who for once came running. Slathering mayonnaise on two pieces of bread, she made herself a turkey sandwich. When she sat down at the table, Gus hunkered over his bowl and ate his tuna.

Her thoughts turned to Jake and what she'd said to him before he'd left.

"But why do you have to go away?" she'd whispered. "I feel guilty running you out of your own house."

"Don't. It's what I do sometimes—when I need to think."

"Think about what?"

"About what the hell we're going to do if you're pregnant."

"What are you saying?" she'd asked.

He'd stopped slinging fishing gear into his backpack and had walked over to her. Cupping her chin with blunt, tanned fingertips so that she was forced to stare up into his blue eyes, he hadn't spoken until he was sure he had her full attention.

"If there's a baby, I want it," he said softly. "Do you understand me?"

But he didn't want her. She'd nodded and after a long moment he'd freed her chin.

"Okay then," he said.

"I could lock myself into the downstairs bedroom and not come out until morning. You wouldn't even know I was here."

He'd turned and smiled at her. "Trust me. It wouldn't be the same. I need to be completely alone."

"But I wouldn't bother you."

"The hell you say. Every fiber in my being would know you're nearby. You bother me by existing."

"Oh."

She must have looked hurt because his expression had gentled.

"But not always in the worst possible way."

Not always in the worst possible way. Was that a compliment?

Before he'd left, he'd locked his office and his bedroom upstairs. She'd stiffened at those final clicks as the bolts shot home and he'd withdrawn his key.

When she'd been a little girl, she used to follow her father everywhere when he'd packed for a trip. She'd lingered, watching him lock all the doors that kept her out of entire wings of their houses and apartments too.

The servants, of course, had had keys so they could clean. But his only daughter had had no access.

All her father's homes had been furnished with valuable antiques and art collections worthy of museums. He'd said he didn't trust the servants to keep her from sitting on the chairs and spilling drinks or food on the furniture or tainting one of his precious sculptures or paintings with oily fingerprints.

How different her mother had been. Their homes had previously been filled with sunlight and flowers and friends. She'd always had time to sit on the floor and play with her daughter or read to her or chat.

After Alicia finished her sandwich, she sat in silence sipping her milk. Finally, she rose and washed the dishes.

Feeling too restless and lonely to shower and get ready for bed, she began to pace, calling to Gus, who had disappeared again.

Climbing the floating stairs, she lingered outside Jake's locked bedroom and remembered the night he'd carried her inside and kicked the door shut. The walls of his bedroom were either floor-to-ceiling bookshelves or tall windows with views of his large backyard and pool.

They'd made love on his bed and then on the thick woven rug by his bed. Then they'd lain in bed talking. When she'd noticed that only books filled his shelves, she'd asked him why he didn't have a single photograph of his friends or family.

"I left home when I was very young. I traveled light. This house is rented, like all the houses I've lived in. So—no pictures."

"You've never built yourself a house?"

"Maybe someday."

"My father didn't like photographs either. He wouldn't even let me have a picture of my mother in my room. He said photographs depressed him because they reminded him of things that were dead and over. He said he wanted to live entirely in the present."

Jake's face had hardened at the mention of her father, but he'd stroked her mouth with a fingertip and had said nothing. Had he known then he would team up with Hayes Daniels the next day and accuse her father? Or had Hayes approached him?

After Jake had blown the whistle on her father, Jake had called her; maybe to explain his side. Or maybe to hear her side.

Not that she'd taken his calls.

Still, how many times had she nearly picked up the phone because she'd ached to hear his voice and had wondered why he was calling?

Part of her wanted to hate him for what he'd done

to her father, but he wasn't her father's only accuser. Serious amounts of money had gone missing. Someone was responsible. Naturally she didn't want to believe it was her father.

Turning, wishing she could empty her mind of all her confusion concerning Jake and her father, Alicia walked back downstairs.

Her footsteps were hollow taps echoing through the house, which felt too empty without Jake.

At the bottom of the stairs she shut her eyes. More than anything she wished he was here.

What was going on?

Never had she felt more mixed up by the impossible, mysterious longings in her heart.

Five

"I told you I was pregnant, didn't I?" Alicia said gloomily. "You should have been prepared."

"*Should have been* is definitely the operative figure of speech here." Jake gripped her elbow and hurriedly propelled her out of the doctor's office building into the parking lot.

It was nearly one o'clock and the heat was searing. Cars whizzed past them on the busy street.

"I didn't realize how much I hoped you were wrong about this," he said, moving to the street side of the walkway to shield her from the traffic.

With an effort, she tried to ignore the sting of his words. She'd hated the way he'd barely looked at her or the doctor, the way he'd barely said a word during the office visit. The instant the doctor had confirmed Alicia's fears, Jake's tanned face had hardened into a stony mask. No matter how the doctor had attempted to get him to open up, he'd rebuffed her every question. The only sign of life in Jake's set face now was the fiery turbulence in his grim blue eyes that hinted at the inner battle raging inside him.

"You certainly put on a happy face in the doctor's office," Jake muttered. "I couldn't believe all the questions you asked the doctor, like this is a normal pregnancy and we are a normal, happy couple."

"I'm not exactly happy," she whispered, warier of him because of his dark mood. "But I wish I was. Just as I wish you could be, too. Any child deserves parents who want him—even ours."

"Hell."

"I can't help it if I want our child to be wanted and have a normal, loving childhood. Any mother would."

"Even a mother who despises the father of her baby?"

But she didn't despise him. She'd liked having him with her at the doctor's office.

"Do you want me to lie to you and your doctor about how I feel?" he continued. "Where will we be if we lie to each other about everything?"

"Where will we be if we concentrate on nothing but how much we hate each other all the time? How can we build on that?"

"What the hell could we possibly build?"

"A positive world for our child."

"I'd say we're off to a damn poor start then."

"Which means we have nowhere to go but up," she said in a whimsical voice that thankfully was too low for him to hear.

"What?"

Unable to deal with his hostile attitude, she said in a louder tone, "Thank you for at least meeting me here.

I really do appreciate it. I was sick again this morning. I wasn't so sure there for a while I'd ever be able to get out of the house."

Her gentle, polite approach calmed him, if only a little.

"I'm sorry you were sick again. It was my idea for you to see a doctor first thing, remember? The least I could do is show up."

"Believe me, some men wouldn't have bothered." *Like her father.*

Jake opened her door of his large, black SUV for her, and she got in. "Fasten your seat belt," he ordered. He waited to make sure she did so before walking around to get in too. Why was his concern about even that small detail such a comfort?

She hated that his doing so registered on such a profound level with her. She was so eager for happiness she grabbed anything positive.

Once he was behind the huge wheel, the woodsy scent of pine, cypress and smoke enveloped her. Strangely, despite the heat, it didn't make her feel the slightest bit sick as some scents did. In fact, he smelled so good, she couldn't resist glancing at him out of the corners of her eyes.

He was so tall and broad shouldered. A lock of dark hair fell across his brow. Why did he have to be so attractive even when he wasn't trying, like now? When he wanted no involvement with her? Dark stubble shadowed his hard jaw and chin and made him look incredibly masculine. He hadn't had time to shower or shave or even to change out of his jeans before their appointment. Shadows ringed his eyes.

He'd obviously been in such a hurry to pick her up

and rush her to the doctor's office, he hadn't bothered about himself at all.

"You look tired," she said, feeling too much unwanted sympathy for him. Yet, even exhausted, he was so virile and utterly male that some feminine, idiotic part of her wanted to swoon over him, despite knowing he probably considered her his enemy.

"Couldn't sleep," he muttered as he leaned forward and started the SUV. He turned on the AC. "Lumpy, stinky mattress. Hot night, too. Couldn't stop thinking about stuff." He shot her an accusing glance and she wondered if concern for her had kept him from sleeping.

He adjusted the air-conditioning. "Is the air okay?"

She nodded.

"What about you? I mean besides the morning sickness." He turned away and pretended to watch the traffic. "You okay? You don't look so perky yourself."

"Couldn't sleep either." Not that she was about to admit to him that she'd tossed and turned because she'd been longing for him all night—because his nearness made her feel safe and secure in ways she'd never known in her whole life. Which was ridiculous, considering the situation.

When his dark head swiveled in her direction, she shyly turned. Under his scowling gaze, her lungs froze.

Suddenly she couldn't breathe. Why did being so close to him in his big vehicle make her so nervous? Why didn't he just drive them home so they weren't trapped in such a small space together with emotions they couldn't deal with? At least on the way she'd have scenery to distract her from him. Now she felt as overwhelmed by him as she had that first night.

"I…I still can't believe this has happened," she said in a low quiet tone.

"I felt like that at first, I mean when Dr. Preston confirmed your fears, but the reality is sinking in pretty fast. You and I are going to have a baby—whether we want it or not. The question is what are going to do to resolve this situation?"

"I haven't thought that far ahead."

"Oh, I bet you have." His deep voice darkened. "You came running to me first thing in need of money, didn't you?"

"No! That's not it. I—I don't want my baby to be illegitimate, that's all."

His dark head jerked toward hers, his blue eyes piercing her. "*That's all?* Surely you're not talking about—marriage?"

She bit her lips and swallowed.

"About you and me…being together…in some sort of permanent arrangement. It's not like this is a hundred years ago and your father's going to follow me down the aisle with a shotgun between my shoulder blades," he said. "Hard to do that under house arrest."

Could she help it if she saw things so simplistically? Every time a teacher at school had asked her to draw a picture of her family, she'd always drawn a mommy and a daddy and herself in the middle.

"You don't actually see us as a couple, do you?" he said.

She shook her head because he so obviously wanted her to. "Look," she said, "I guess I just panicked and thought when I felt so sick that I couldn't do this alone. Maybe I would have been stronger before…but now… I have no money. No allies. No family really…other than Daddy, who's been indicted."

"And you're so used to money, you don't know how to get by without it."

"My life hasn't been what you think. I don't believe I have any friends left in Louisiana. Everybody here blames me for what they think Daddy did."

"*Because of what he did!* And what you helped him do in all probability. Whose fault is that?"

"Right. You think I schemed to steal millions of dollars from Houses for Hurricane Victims and his bank? And that I deliberately set out to destroy your good name?"

"Well, your father damn sure did, that's for sure."

"I think my father's innocent."

"Then where's the money he managed? Why can't we find any records to prove he ever invested a single dollar? Maybe you don't know how the charity world operates, so I'll fill you in on a little secret. At the first hint of scandal, all future funding dries up. So now poor families, who were counting on me to build them homes, won't get them. Because of my close association to the charity, funding for my architectural projects is drying up as well. It would be financial suicide for me to associate myself with you right now. And now you want me to marry you?"

"The government has been investigating him for the past six weeks, and so far they've found nothing to link me to any of it. Doesn't that tell you anything about me? I never volunteered for that organization. I never worked at Daddy's bank or the shipyard either."

"Maybe you're good at covering your tracks."

"Or maybe I'm innocent. I was an editor and a writer."

"I wasn't born yesterday. You got that job because of your father's connections."

"Maybe."

"Maybe you're a taker like your father. Maybe you came to me yesterday hoping I'd help you financially."

"Is everything really just money to you?"

He leaned toward her. "How dare *you* ask *me* that?"

"Then what about our child? I want our baby to have his or her father's name…and his love, if that's possible. Your love. That's very important to me. Do you want to play a role in his or her life, or not?"

He was silent.

"Because if you don't, one of my oldest and dearest friends lives in London. Her name's Carol Lawton, and when she heard about my problems, she offered me a job in a publishing firm over there. It would mean leaving Louisiana…"

"No!"

"You wouldn't have to stay married to me for very long to give him his name. You could even tell people why you had to marry me."

"No. I couldn't do that." He hesitated, his gaze sweeping her. "So, what kind of theoretical marriage do you imagine we could possibly have? Hell, the only plus we have going for us is that we're great together in bed."

"No sex," she asserted in a low, breathy rush.

"What? You expect me to tie myself to you without even that as a fringe benefit?" He stared through her. "What about you? After the way you kissed me yesterday, are you sure that's what you want?"

"Who are you kidding? You ran off to the swamp yesterday because you couldn't take the heat from that kiss. Our marriage should be about the baby—not us. I, for one—definitely—don't think we should complicate our confusing situation with more sex."

"Definitely?" The edges of his tense mouth relaxed. "You sound so…er…determined."

She wished. Who was she kidding? Jake had such a devastating effect on her, she wondered if she'd be able to resist him if he chose to exploit that weakness some night when she was feeling particularly lonely and unloved.

"So, we're talking about a marriage of convenience. Doubtless, you'll demand a sizable settlement when we split up?" he said.

"No settlement."

"Right. A Butler who isn't after my money. What a refreshing development."

"I'll sign a prenup if you want me to. If you help me find a job somewhere…or help me get started in London, that would be wonderful. We…we wouldn't even have to live together while we're married either. I just want the baby to feel his father wanted him."

"So, no sex and no settlement, huh?"

"I told you, this isn't about sex or money. It's about what's best for the baby. I grew up with all the money in the world, but…"

"But with a real bastard for a father, who never gave a damn about you. Poor little rich girl."

"Please…don't run him down." She stopped, feeling bleak at the dark feelings his words too easily stirred within her. Her childhood with her father may have been loveless, but that didn't mean she could bear other people sitting in judgment of him. Especially not now when he was under house arrest and she herself was uncertain as to his guilt of innocence.

Turning away so he wouldn't read the longing that

welled up inside her, she watched a happy young couple leave the medical building. They were laughing and holding hands. When they reached their battered, compact car, the man pulled the woman into his arms and kissed her fervently. Maybe they, too, had learned they were going to have a baby—only they were both thrilled.

Color me green, she thought.

Watching them, too, Jake stiffened. "Sorry…for what I just said about your dad," he said in a gentler tone.

"It's okay," she whispered. "Our marriage would hardly be a fairy tale with the promise of happily-ever-after like we both dreamed we might know with someone we would have freely chosen some day. And believe me, my father won't be happy about any of this when he finds out."

"If you're determined to get married, we live together," Jake growled.

"Why—when you didn't even want to spend the night with me last night?"

"Who the hell knows? Maybe because I don't trust you as far as I can throw you. As long as you're my wife, I'll keep you close so I can keep an eye on you. Besides, who'll look after you if I'm not around?"

Against her better judgment, at this softer sentiment her heart warmed to him a little.

"My house is big," he said. "You can use the bedroom downstairs that you slept in last night. I'll live on the second floor just like always. But while we're married, you're to have nothing to do with your father."

"But Jake…."

"That's nonnegotiable. I don't trust him or you—and I especially don't trust the two of you together."

"But, he's been arrested. He's alone and in trouble.

I know how that feels. I can't just turn my back on him."

"No involvement. So long as you're my wife, you're not to associate with him. Not even a phone call. You're to stay away from his trial, too. Do you understand me?"

She turned and stared mutely out the window at the cars speeding by beyond the parking lot. What if her father was innocent and she deserted him?

"Do you want to marry me or not?" Jake demanded, hard finality in his voice.

Uncertain, she froze. Finally she nodded. "But only for the baby's sake."

He frowned. "Then you'll agree to stay away from him while we're married?"

"Yes," she whispered in a tone that was so faint it was nearly inaudible.

"There can be no other men in your life while we're married."

"What?" she murmured, feeling crushed that he thought her so low. But then, all he knew was that she'd made love to him the first night she'd met him. How could he possibly realize how special he'd been, how profoundly connected she'd felt to him?

"Since our marriage will upset a lot of people, including my clients and employees, I want it to appear respectable. I don't want to give the press or your numerous enemies anything extra to chew on. So you'll have to agree not to be seen out with other men."

"Of course," she said quietly even as anger began to bubble inside her. "What about you, Mr. High And Mighty? Will the same rule apply to you?"

"I will abide by the same rule—for the same reason."

"Not out of any loyalty to me. But then, why should you feel the slightest loyalty? You don't want to marry me any more than I want to marry you."

"Maybe we're finally beginning to understand each other. Will you be faithful?"

"I said yes already!" she snapped. "Did you really spend the night alone last night?"

He smiled. "So you care a little, too?"

She shook her head much too vigorously, because his quick white smile, the beautiful smile that had seduced her, broadened, causing her blood to heat.

"Were you really alone?" she persisted, furious at him for being so attractive to her just because of a smile and at herself for being so susceptible to his virile brand of sexiness.

"I was. So, when you're my wife, a wife who, for the record, refuses to sleep with me, will you expect me to answer questions like that if I choose not to come home some night?"

"Look…I shouldn't have asked about last night. Forget I did it! I don't care what you do…."

"Okay." Grinning, he held up his hands in a gesture of mock innocence. "But just in case you do care…a tiny bit…I spent the night alone like I said. I was in a houseboat in the swamp behind Belle Rose that I told you about. The only time I left it was when I built a fire on a muddy bank and cooked out."

"What did you cook?"

"A squirrel. There's not much to a squirrel. So it was a long, hungry night spent *alone*."

She frowned. "You killed a little squirrel?"

"I threw my knife. He died in a flash."

"I can't believe you'd be so cruel!"

"What? Do you think I like killing animals? I like to

eat. Do you think you're morally superior because your meat comes in plastic-covered packages in the grocery store?"

Unable to refute his logic but not liking the thought of him eating a helpless, little squirrel any better than she originally had, she began to twirl a strand of her hair and fume as she stared into the distance.

"Look, I had to get away," he said. "Firing everybody… you showing up saying you might be pregnant…was too much for one day. I didn't want to be with you…or any other woman. I know it sounds unusual, going off alone into the wilderness on the spur of the moment, but it's something I do fairly frequently when I need to chill. I'll probably do it again during our marriage—if we're married any time. Happy now?"

"I wish."

"Okay. Back to the plan. We marry. At some point after our child is born, we go our separate ways. No settlement. Just custody arrangements."

"Fine," she agreed, feeling dismal at that prospect.

"That's all you really want?"

"I don't want any of this!"

"You wanted me *that* night," he reminded her.

The memory of it, plus the knowledge that she still wanted him, was not her favorite fun fact.

"You knew how desperate I felt that night…because my father had just told me he was caught in a credit crunch and was on the verge of losing everything, including the bank, if the merger between his shipyard and Claiborne Energy didn't work out."

He nodded.

Knowing that she'd had a date with Logan that night to his grandfather's eightieth birthday, her father had ordered her to do everything in her power to charm

Logan and lull his suspicions that anything might be amiss with the Butler empire. But Logan had been interested only in Cici.

"I felt shy that night at Belle Rose when Logan abandoned me to dance with Cici. I didn't know anyone. Then you started smiling at me from across the room. I smiled back and you came up to me and were so nice, I began to enjoy myself and open up. When you said you were involved with my father in that charity, I told you how worried I was about him. I had no idea you were planning to gang up with Hayes Daniels and accuse him of all those crimes or that maybe the only reason you took an interest in me was to get more information out of me."

"I wasn't planning anything. I had no idea your father was guilty of anything that night. Cici simply wanted to spend time with Logan, and she asked me to take care of you. Hayes didn't clue me in about Mitchell until the next morning. But after the credit problems you'd hinted your father was having, I thought you must have known everything your father was doing and that you were involved. So I was furious at you for deceiving me…and seducing me. I thought maybe you did all that in an effort to buy my silence where your father was concerned. I called you because I wanted to give you a chance to defend yourself. When you wouldn't take my calls, I took that to mean you were guilty."

She hadn't answered the phone because she'd thought him the most treacherous human being alive for seducing her to gain information about her father.

"I was very lonely that night, too," he said. "Being with my family always makes me feel like I don't know my place in the world. Then Logan abandoned you. And you were very, very beautiful."

She blushed, feeling shyly pleased.

"You weren't what I was expecting," he said. "I thought you'd be more like your father but you were nothing like him. You swept me off my feet, as you probably know."

Had he felt the same incredible rush of thrilling excitement in her presence she'd found in his? She wanted to believe that so much.

"Later I wondered if you'd been setting me up," Jake said, killing the softness she'd been feeling toward him. "What about this pregnancy? Did you get pregnant on purpose? Maybe to buy me off?"

"You have to know I didn't. I would never deliberately bring a baby into a mess like this! You seemed so nice that night, and idiot that I was, I trusted you enough to confide in you…and sleep with you."

He stared into her eyes for a long time.

"Okay," he muttered as he finally put the SUV into gear and pulled out into traffic. "Okay."

"The morning after we slept together my father called me and told me about the missing money from the Houses for Hurricane Victims. He said you took it, and that you set him up."

"Well, I didn't. So do you always believe everything your father says?"

"I try to see his side of things…because he's my father and the only parent I have left."

"Look," he growled, "I was nice to you that night because… Hell, I already told you why…." He swore under his breath. "If I'm already damned in your eyes, why should I bother to defend myself?"

After that final question, the thick silence that fell between them grew increasingly strained.

Her mind drifted, and she remembered all too well

how Jake had coaxed her to confide in him their first night together. He'd pretended to listen to her fears concerning her father and to understand; pretended to care about her, and, she, as always, too eager and made happy by any kindness, however small, had ended up in his bed.

But not before she'd told him too much. Pretending sympathy and passion after her confidences, Jake had soothingly kissed her mouth, her face, her throat, her breasts, until he'd made her feel safe and breathless with desire for him.

"It's going to be all right," he'd whispered in a kindly tone. "Dark moments are part of life. They teach us lessons we need to learn."

Soon she'd been clinging, longing for more than his compassion. Forgetting her father and his troubles, she'd begged Jake to make love to her and he'd complied, showering her with all the warmth and passion she'd craved.

Then the next morning Jake had gone out. Later her father had called her and cruelly informed her that the merger was in trouble—and that Jake Claiborne, along with Hayes Daniels, Logan's CEO, had joined forces and reported him to the feds.

Her father and his bank and shipyard had gone down in flames, and Jake was at least partially responsible. Every time she'd thought of how she'd bared her soul and given her body to a man who'd spent the night with her, maybe to milk her for information about her father she'd felt freshly used and humiliated. She'd told herself she shouldn't ever see Jake again or even take his calls.

Not so easy when he'd continued to call her and all her friends had cut her dead.

Most of the time she'd ignored his calls, but once

when he'd phoned her after some particularly vicious stories about her had filled the Internet and newspapers, she'd actually wanted to hear his voice so much she'd answered. They'd soon quarreled, but she'd had the feeling he'd been concerned about her. Then she'd seen him at Logan's wedding. Not that they'd spoken.

She forced her mind back to the present and their new reality. Jake was driving so fast, she was clutching the armrest while houses and strip malls flew by in a blur. When they reached his sprawling home, half a dozen reporters' vans were still lined up in front of his house.

Van doors popped open and reporters rushed toward his SUV as he swerved into his drive. Ignoring them, Jake drove the large vehicle slowly toward a gate that opened electronically and then shut behind them, locking out the invasive horde.

In his garage Jake cut the engine and turned slowly to face her. "Okay, you told me what you want and what you think about me, didn't you?"

"I guess," she replied.

"So, here's what I want out of this disastrous affair. First, we involve as few people as possible in our little scheme. I don't want my grandfather hurt. I'm not on the easiest terms with Logan or his new wife, Cici, so the less they know about this, the better. My grandfather's lonely. I don't want him forming an unsuitable attachment to a woman I don't plan to keep in my life any longer than necessary."

"But he was so friendly to me at his party. Do you really want me to be rude to him?"

"Be polite but cool. In case you didn't realize it, you're natural at that role."

"Thanks…for nothing," she whispered.

"Not for nothing, sweetheart. I agreed to marry you, didn't I? For me—that's a big step."

"For me, too," she said.

His weary expression told her he didn't believe her. "You…proposed."

"Not because I wanted to," she flared.

"So—I guess the next step is to plan our wedding. Are you up to that or do you want me to get Vanessa to handle it?"

As a child her mother had let her decorate for all her parties. Excitedly they'd cut out cardboard stars and glued glitter on them. They'd hung posters and sent out invitations. Once her mother had rented ponies and Alicia and all her friends had ridden in the back yard. But after her mother's death, the celebration of Alicia's birthdays, when remembered, and of the important milestones in her life had always been planned by her father's employees.

No way was she going to let her wedding, such as it was, be planned by Jake's office staff.

"I'll plan it," she whispered, hurt beyond words that he'd suggested such a thing even though she knew her feelings were utterly illogical.

Pregnancy. Hormones. A marriage of convenience to Jake. She was definitely in for a roller-coaster ride.

Six

How ironic that St. Anthony's Garden, the spot his bride had chosen for their wedding, had once been the most popular dueling ground in New Orleans. Too bad the twenty-first century was more civilized. If Jake could have called his bride's father out and shot him, he would have.

Tonight peace reigned. Birds chirped high in the oak trees. A great sculpture of the Sacred Heart reigned in the shady nook that smelled so sweetly of olives. Beyond the garden, tourists chattered as they posed in Pirate's Alley snapping pictures. In the distance street musicians played jazz.

Jake wanted to hate Alicia for complicating his life but reason told him he was equally to blame. He didn't want to marry her, but with every word that the priest uttered binding him to Alicia Butler, his desire for her grew until it felt like a crushing weight. Indeed, ever since he'd agreed to the marriage, thoughts of a naked and eagerly writhing Alicia in his bed had consumed him. All night long he'd lain awake in his bed and thought of her lying in hers downstairs, and he'd wondered if she was thinking of him.

Why did she have to stand so close to him in the dense, humid air so that with every breath he inhaled her perfume?

They say a little piece of paper doesn't matter; that it changes nothing.

They don't know crap. He felt trapped—doomed. At the same time his body raged to have her again. And again. He burned as if he had a fever. His feelings for this woman were illogical and out of proportion to any he'd ever felt for another.

Get a grip.

To distract himself Jake stared up at the triple spires of St. Louis Cathedral towering above their small wedding party hunched together beneath the hurricane-damaged trees. The only guests were his secretary and her bored-looking son, whose dark head was bent over some electronic device.

Thankfully, no member of his own family or Alicia's was present to witness this farce.

It didn't console him that Alicia seemed equally miserable. Her slim fingers that gripped his arm for support shook. Her carriage was rigid; her lovely face ashen.

His heart caught. Why should he sympathize? With a little imagination, surely she could have dreamed up a better solution than a sexless marriage that was already driving him crazy.

A man forced into a shotgun marriage should get

something for his trouble, Jake thought gloomily. Why had he stupidly agreed not to sleep with her?

He'd been sober, that was why. He never thought straight sober.

Too bad he wasn't sober now. Thanks to the shots of whiskey he'd drunk to give him the courage to show up, he felt dangerously near some breaking point.

The late-evening sunlight sifting through the oaks caressed her high, classic brow and made her creamy skin glow. Every time their glances met, her large, dark eyes shot sparks. Why did she keep licking her plump, sensual mouth? Didn't she know that the sight of her tongue had him remembering all the erotic places her moist lips and tongue had touched him with deft little strokes?

His gaze drifted over her straight chiseled nose, her delicate chin and her long graceful neck. Her white lace sheath was skintight, showing off her flawless figure even as the purity of its color made her look virginal. How could a pregnant woman whose breasts were swollen look so untouched and sexy?

Hell.

"Jake, will you have this woman to be your wedded wife, to love her, comfort her, honor and keep her, forsaking all others, so long as you both shall live?" Father Alex asked.

Alicia's hot, dark eyes flashed when they met Jake's again, causing his blood to quicken.

"I will," he whispered hoarsely through clenched teeth.

No matter how he fought to blank out her soft response as she pledged herself to him forever, when her husky voice said, "I will," something shifted inside him and the dark need to claim her obsessed him all over again.

Suddenly he couldn't wait to slip his ring on her finger. He didn't want other men looking at her or touching her without knowing who she belonged to.

She was his wife. His. Period.

As the priest continued to drone, Jake's blood buzzed with fierce passion. Damn it, he wanted to at least kiss her. Wasn't that part of this hellish ceremony?

After an interminable amount of sanctimonious verbiage, the priest finally pronounced them man and wife. "You may kiss your bride," he said.

In a flutter, Alicia tried to turn away, but Jake grabbed her slim wrist and spun her into his hard arms. Cutting off her startled cry of protest, he claimed her mouth with his.

Her hands came up to push against his wide chest, but at the first touch of his lips, she sighed and then whispered his name.

"Jake, oh, Jake…" Her dark eyes were aflame with needs as deep and dark as his own. Rising onto her tiptoes, her arms circling his neck, she clung, leaning into his body.

She was soft and warm. Waves of hot pleasure washed through him. Her lips parted, inviting more.

Maybe everything about their marriage was wrong, but this felt right. Too right.

She was shaking, and so was he as his tongue swept inside her warm, honeyed mouth.

His kiss was needlessly aggressive, possessive and primitive. Once he'd started kissing her, some force outside him took over, and he couldn't stop himself.

He'd married her, hadn't he? She was his. If his pulse

had been racing before the kiss, her satiny mouth and honeyed taste made it accelerate to rocket speed.

Ever since he'd kissed her that afternoon she'd shown up on his doorstep, he'd thought about doing it again, thought about it too damn much. The night he'd spent in the swamp to get his head straight had changed nothing.

His arms crushed her body to his. He wanted her to moan, to press her slim body and heavy breasts closer, and to go limp and beg. The longer he kissed her, the more he wanted from her.

"Jake, we're in public," she whispered shyly. Her slender hands fells away from his neck and wedged themselves between their bodies. Pushing against him, she stared up at him with eyes filled with a mixture of longing and embarrassment.

Slowly her puny efforts penetrated his lust-charged brain, and he realized he was way out of line.

What the hell was he doing? Cursing his damnable weakness for her, he let her go and pivoted free.

Blushing, Alicia fell back a few feet. Turning her back to him, she wiped her mouth and smoothed her hair with hands that trembled.

When Vanessa's sharp, questioning gaze sought his, he felt like an idiot, so he scowled back at her, willing to keep her damn mouth shut and mind her own business for once. She did, but her expression softened as she regarded first him and then his wife.

Then he realized Vanessa wasn't the only member of their little party who was gazing at them with rapt fascination. Her son had stopped playing with his electronic device, and Father Alex had dropped his Bible and looked agitated as he stooped to pick it up.

Feeling a growing pressure to say something or do

something, he turned on Alicia. "Well, now that we've gotten the ceremony out of the way, Vanessa can drive you home. I'm going back to my office."

Alicia's cheeks flamed with wounded pride. "But it's Saturday."

"So?"

"But...I mean...when will you be home?"

He didn't want her to know how profoundly she affected him. He didn't want any of them to know.

"This is hardly a real marriage," he said beneath his breath. "So don't wait up. Watch a movie. Read a book. Pet the beast. Frankly, I don't care what you do."

She turned so white, he was afraid she'd faint. He was reaching for her when Vanessa rushed to her side.

More than anything he wanted to take Alicia in his arms again. He wanted to drive her home and spend the night with her, but his feelings were too raw and charged.

His bride's stricken expression made him feel like a heel. He'd hurt her, and he felt bad about that, too.

How the hell had she turned the tables on him? Her father had stolen money from his charity and from thousands of other innocent people. She was probably in on the entire scam.

But was she?

Damn it. Fool that he was, he very much wanted to believe she was innocent.

"Some honeymoon, huh?" Vanessa smiled as she stood on Jake's front porch. "I'd come in and stay for a while if I didn't have Rick in the car."

"I'll be fine."

"Look, I don't know what's going on with my boss, and I don't really know you, other than what I've read, but if you feel like talking to somebody, remember my home phone is number two on your speed dial. I'll be home with the kids all evening." Vanessa smiled at her.

"Thanks." Just knowing that someone was out there was reassuring. "And thanks for coming today," Alicia said. "I…I always dreamed of a different kind of wedding."

"Don't we all? I had a great wedding and a lousy marriage. Maybe you'll have the reverse. It could happen. Jake's a good man, better than most—but he is a man. Sure, he has his limitations. Trust me, he already had a lot on his plate before you showed up on his doorstep."

"I know. And he thinks it's all my fault."

"I'm beginning to doubt that. You hang in there… and he'll see you for who you really are. Be patient…. Oh, who am I to talk? I'm really the last thing from a romantic."

Vanessa reached for her and pulled her into her arms. After hugging her, she whispered, "Good luck. You deserve it. For what it's worth, you were a very beautiful bride. I think you knocked Jake off his feet. He'll be back, probably sooner than you expect."

"You'd better be calling to tell me you didn't go through with it!" Mitchell roared.

Alicia sagged against a wall as she gripped the telephone. A small voice did ask why he couldn't once take her side. Vanessa, who didn't even know her, was at least trying not judge her.

"But Daddy…."

In spite of the fact that Jake had forbidden her to call her father, she had. While Jake had been at work, she'd left her father a message yesterday informing him of her intention to marry Jake today. Besides, what was the harm? She hadn't told him where or when, so it wasn't as if she'd invited him and he might show up and upset Jake or anything.

As was his custom, Mitchell hadn't even bothered to return her call in a timely fashion.

"So you married him?"

"I called because I didn't want you learn about it by reading it in the newspapers or on the Web."

"As if it matters how I learn it! Where is he now? Is he listening? Gloating?"

"No. He left…right after the marriage ceremony. I don't know where he is or if he's ever coming home. It's not like he wanted to marry me."

"What? Then why the hell… Never mind! It's your funeral. You were a fool to marry him, so you deserve whatever misery he dishes out—which will be plenty, I assure you. You made your bed—now lie in it!" With that her father, who wasn't known for his patience or gentleness, hung up on her, leaving her alone in Jake's big house to enjoy what was left of her wedding day.

As if she could enjoy anything now, trapped in this house, knowing she'd married a man who didn't care for her, knowing that by doing so, she'd turned her father completely against her. She should have realized how totally empty and bereft she'd feel once she truly alienated him.

Laying down her cordless phone, she went in search of Gus. Naturally, he wouldn't come or even mew when she called. When she couldn't find him anywhere on the first floor, she climbed the stairs and found him reclining in the hall outside Jake's locked, bedroom door, thumping his tail while waiting for the master of the house to come home.

"You little traitor. You're worthless sometimes, you know that?"

Gus's eyes remained shut. He looked much too serene as his head remained on his crossed paws even as his tail began to twitch faster.

When she leaned down and picked him up, he meowed loudly and swished his tail to show that he was very much annoyed.

"Traitor! You're my cat, you know, not his," she said, kissing the tip of his ear.

The ear whipped against his skull as she headed down the stairs with him. His yellow eyes stared into hers with a feral look that said he didn't know any such thing. He was his own cat, thank you very much, and, of course, he refused to purr and began to strain to get away.

When she reached the bottom floor, he twisted sharply. A claw from a back paw caught in her forearm as he jumped to the floor. Then he leaped back up the stairs, no doubt to resume his stubborn vigil outside Jake's door.

"He doesn't want you any more than he wants me, you know," she yelled. "Maybe less!" Then she stalked to the hall bathroom, and washed off the beads of blood and toweled her arm dry.

What had she done? Why had she ever thought marrying Jake even for a short time would be a solution to anything? She'd completely alienated her father now, and that loss filled her with a mixture of guilt and regret. Maybe he hadn't been the most attentive of fathers but he'd always been there, at least in the background. Until now.

He was probably going to prison and she'd married the man who was responsible. Tears flooded her eyes but she brushed them aside, refusing to surrender to emotional turmoil or self-doubt. She'd done what she had to do for her baby.

Marching into the kitchen, she poured herself a glass of ice water and then gobbled three dill pickles and a slice of cheese. Then she hurried to her bedroom where she undressed and got ready for a long evening of watching television and reading the books and magazines on her nightstand. All of Jake's magazines had to do with outdoor adventures, especially in Alaska, which sounded like a freezing hell with way too many mosquitoes, not to mention bears. Funny, but hadn't he told her that first night that he sometimes went there to be all alone when he was feeling most stressed?

Later, as she climbed into the big bed all by herself and pulled the sheets up to her neck, loneliness washed over her. She wanted Jake, which was stupid and illogical, considering their circumstances. He had kissed her, yes. Passionately. And then he'd hated them both for it.

Why should she think she could matter to Jake, her father's enemy, who'd been forced to marry her, when she hadn't ever mattered to anyone else before? Not even her own father.

Except Mother.

Don't think about any of that. Or even the present. You will get through this. Concentrate on the future.

Thinking of her own baby, her spirits gradually brightened. She wanted her child fiercely and she was willing to fight for the best possible life for her baby—and that included giving her baby a father. Like her mother, she would create a beautiful nursery. Like her mother, she would spend as much time as possible with her child. And maybe…maybe in time what her father had done or hadn't done would become clear. And Jake's attitude toward her and their child would change.

For no reason at all she remembered how he'd held her hand and listened so intently that first night she'd confided in him. Then he'd taken her in his arms the day she'd shown up on his doorstep and told him she was pregnant. Today he'd kissed her passionately. Maybe it wasn't so foolish to believe he had it in him to make a wonderful father and even a good husband.

She had to hold on to that possibility…and fight for it.

Seven

Alicia woke the next morning feeling stronger—until she caught the thick scent of boudin sausage, frying eggs and steaming chicory-flavored coffee wafting out of the air-conditioning vent.

Obviously Jake had come home. Smiling because she was glad he was home, she sat up. At that slight movement her stomach became hollow and her mouth was suddenly too dry for her to swallow. Throwing her sheets aside, she rushed for the bathroom, intending to splash cold water on her face.

In her haste, she slammed into a low table. The china teacup and saucer she'd forgotten to return to the kitchen last night shattered on the oak floor. With a little cry, she kept running.

After bathing her face, the nausea gradually passed.

Last night to cheer herself up she'd watched a couple of comedies on television, which had eased her depression and caused her to laugh until she'd nearly cried. She'd fallen asleep feeling more hopeful about the future.

At the sound of the bedroom door opening and closing and heavy, male footsteps approaching, she turned slowly.

"Jake?"

"Who else? Are you all right?" he rumbled in his deep, insistent voice.

"Just a touch of morning sickness, but I'm fine. Or at least I will be…soon," she whispered. "Give me a minute. I don't want you to see me like this."

"Are you naked again?" He sounded hopeful.

"You would think of that."

"I'm a man. You're a beautiful woman, who's now my wife. A woman I have a sexual history with. Of course I imagine you naked. All the time."

"Beautiful? I haven't brushed my hair and I've got mascara smudged under my eyes." She groaned.

"I was just trying to make you forget how rotten you feel."

"Just go away."

Then he was there beside her with the disloyal Gus Dear close at his heels. The feline devil had the gall to purr as his black tail curled around Jake's legs and then hers.

"Please leave me—both of you," she begged even as Jake's hand against her back and Gus's silky tail raised goose bumps. "I'll be okay. Really! Go eat your sausage…and give Gus some tuna or something. Oh, God, tuna!" At the thought of tuna, she fought to swallow.

"So it was the smell of our breakfast that made you feel sick."

"Partly, but I just wake up that way a lot of mornings."

"I'm sorry. I shouldn't have left you alone last night."

Jake turned on the faucet, wet a rag and then shut it off. His arms circled her waist gently and he bathed her warm face and lips with a cool rag while Gus's intent yellow eyes watched them both.

"How did you even know I felt queasy?"

"I heard a sound and wanted to make sure you were all right."

"Probably the cup I broke when I ran in here. I'm sorry—"

"Forget it. I'll sweep it up in a minute."

"You must have been very late last night," she said, finally looking up at him. Where was her pride? Why had she admitted she'd even noticed the hour?

His icy blue eyes were shadowed, with exhaustion she thought, and his dark face looked ravaged.

"Yes, I was late. Your light was out. I didn't think you heard me come in."

She wasn't about to admit that she hadn't, even though after her comedies she'd lain alone in the dark for hours listening to every sound the mansion had made. How had she missed his return?

"I didn't want to bother you," he said.

Not for the first time she wondered why he had insisted that they live together if her mere presence was such a torture to him he couldn't stand to be in the same house with her.

"I didn't get much sleep because your cat insisted on sleeping with me."

"You should have locked him out then."

"I did, but he yowled and scratched at my door until

I let him back in. Then he lay on top of me purring for the rest of the night."

"I tried to coax him downstairs to sleep with me earlier but I'm afraid he insisted on lying in wait for you outside your door."

"Stubborn creatures, cats," Jake said.

"Disloyal!" she snapped.

"They know what they want, and they never give up."

Jake's hard glance sought her face and then raked her body, causing confused emotions to course through her. Then he smiled. "I have a feeling he's going to make a real nuisance of himself while we're married. Funny thing—I sort of enjoyed his company last night. I didn't feel like sleeping alone."

If Gus was winning him so easily maybe there was a chance for her....

A chance for what, you fool? This isn't a real marriage. Jake's lost lots of money and his reputation is in shreds. He blames you. Daddy's been indicted because of him. You can't forget any of that—ever!

And yet people dealt with crises and moved on, didn't they?

"I'm all right now, so you can go," she whispered, struggling to stand.

"Are you sure?" he asked.

The warmth of his hands lingered so caressingly on her arms that she was almost seduced into allowing herself the pleasure of his touch. Then she remembered how he'd cut her at their wedding and left her alone all last night. Shakily, she drew herself up taller and pushed his hands away.

"I know you don't like me," she said.

"Is this your perverse way of seeking a compliment?"

"No! Of course not!"

"I think it is, so I'll have to dream one up." He scratched his dark head.

If she didn't know better, she would have thought his quick smile endearingly tender.

"You make it sound like that's very difficult to do."

His hand touched the back of her waist gently and then brushed her fingertips. "Not so difficult as you might think. It's impossible to hate you, *cher*...knowing that you are carrying my child," he murmured.

He squeezed her hand. "You were very beautiful yesterday. Okay. Enough compliments." Then he threw his dark head back and laughed. "Be a good girl. It's early. Quit looking for trouble. Take a shower and comb your hair. You'll feel better, and maybe you won't be so set on bringing out the worst in me—which is fairly easy for you to do—as I'm sure you know."

Thirty minutes later a freshly showered Alicia walked into the kitchen and was surprised to find her husband sprawled at the table in crisp, pressed jeans and a white shirt, looking much too relaxed and handsome with his cup of coffee as he read the paper.

He'd eaten, washed his dishes and cooking utensils and put them away. So why was her husband, who preferred to avoid her, still hanging out in his tidy kitchen? Surely he wasn't eagerly waiting for his temporary bride to appear.

Sunshine streamed through the windows, filling the mostly white room with golden light. He looked so content with his dark head bent over his paper, for a second she could almost forget how angrily he'd loomed beside her at their wedding yesterday before vanishing on their wedding night. She could almost imagine herself a happy bride.

Then their reality slammed her anew. He was her sworn enemy. Kindness from him was not to be counted on or treasured. It was to be distrusted. Thus, when he looked up at her with an amiable smile on his dark face, she frowned.

"What?" He sat up straighter and finger-combed his dark hair. "Am I guilty of some awful new crime or do I just have a crumb on my lip? Or nose?"

As he brushed his mouth and nose with his napkin, she laughed in spite of herself.

"No."

"You want me gone so you can have the kitchen to yourself? Well, I won't be bullied out of my own house."

"I assumed you'd be at the office, avoiding me again…like last night," she said.

"Right," he said, "we're the weirdo newlyweds who did some very interesting variations on sex—positions that are probably still illegal in some states—on this very table, but now we are supposed to have an aversion to sex."

Maybe because he was so preoccupied with sex or the lack of it, she remembered lying naked on the kitchen table in this very room, crying out his name in the heat of her passion. She'd loved him that night, incoherently. With his every touch, with every flick of his tongue, he'd awakened a fire inside her she hadn't known existed, and the embers of that fire still hadn't gone out.

As he stared at the table, she began to sizzle.

Sensing an advantage when she blushed, he moved his hand back and forth across the smooth finish of the tabletop in the way he might stroke a woman. "You know you could change your mind about that. I won't object."

"But you don't even like me."

"I'm a man." He ran his hand along the tabletop again, caressing it. "I can compartmentalize. Let's just say my body likes yours, and it wonders…upon occasion… rather frequently—hell, all the time—how yours feels about mine. If you want the truth, I don't think I slept a wink last night. I kept thinking of you in your bed and me upstairs sleeping with a cat."

She moved to set a kettle boiling on the stove. "You make us sound like we're no better than animals."

"You're in my house, cute as hell…available. I wouldn't be normal if you didn't tempt me."

"Even though you hate my father?"

"*He* isn't here. With any luck he'll be sent to a place where he can't hurt any more people."

Fortunately, the tea kettle whistled. With hands that shook she pulled an egg out of the fridge and placed it in the middle of a pot. As she poured boiling water over it, the egg cracked. She set the pot on the stove top anyway. She was almost glad he'd reminded her of her father's plight and the satisfaction he took in it. The knowledge helped her build up her defenses.

"I'm just being honest," he said. "There's a bit of the wild in us all. Why else do we have to spend years and years civilizing our young? Why else did we behave like we did *that* night? On this very table?"

"Stop…."

"You brought out the beast. I think you liked it, too. In fact, I know you did."

She wet her lips with her tongue and was too aware of his avid eyes glued to her moist lips. For six weeks she'd been a virtual prisoner in her apartment, hated by all. Loneliness and the desire for companionship had built into an almost palpable need. If he stuck around in the same room where she'd been so crazy to have him, saying he wanted her, she wasn't sure how well she'd control her attraction for him.

"Can we please please change the subject?" she pleaded.

Newspapers rustled as he set his paper aside. "You mean…from sex?" he murmured thickly.

Afraid he'd see her flushed cheeks again and understand just how much he affected her, she kept her back to him. "Yes."

"Okay," he muttered. "Sure. Hey, here's some good news for you that has nothing to do with sex. Nowhere in this newspaper did I see any mention of our marriage. Looks like we're still flying under the radar. When people find out, I'll be bombarded at the office. No telling who else will fire me."

"I'm sorry for ruining your life. If you've finished your own breakfast, you don't have to stay here just to entertain me, you know," she whispered.

"I wanted to discuss a few more things—other than sex."

The word sent more tingles through her. "Grrrr."

He laughed. "I think you're running as hot as I am. Maybe hotter."

"What things did you want to discuss?" she said through gritted teeth, too hatefully aware of her heart racing.

"For starters, tomorrow I want to make some financial arrangements for you. Open a new account you can sign on, so you won't feel so dependent on me."

"Why would you do that when I imagine you want

revenge for all those crimes you believe my father and I committed against you?"

"I didn't dream up what you or your father did, so I'm under no illusions about your character. Or his. *Especially his.* But like you pointed out, you have no money or allies. You're my wife and you're carrying my baby. You need to buy things for yourself and our baby."

"I couldn't possibly accept—"

"Anything from me—the enemy." His lips had tightened. "I'm afraid you'll have to. What choice do either of us have? Much as I might want to treat you like a pauper, it would make me look bad. Much as you want to treat me as the enemy, you have no one else who cares as much as I do.

"Our baby needs a nursery. Supplies. A baby bed. God only knows what else. Am I right?"

She sighed. "I do want to create a charming nursery. I guess since I always had money, I never thought much about it. My job as an editor didn't pay much, but it didn't matter. I loved writing and editing, and I could rely on the trust fund money. So, now that the money's all gone, I've got to get used to a new way of living. And thinking. I'll need to think about a career."

"True. But not now. Until the baby's born, I'm going to take care of you. And the baby. That's final."

"Do your people always do what you say, when you say?"

"You're my wife. My broke, pregnant wife. You're my responsibility. You don't have a choice. Why is that so difficult for you to grasp?"

"Maybe because ours is the last thing from a real marriage."

"Right. So, let's be sure and make ourselves just as

miserable as we can at every possible opportunity. Is that your goal?"

No, this morning she just wanted to stay out of his arms…and his bed. His talking about sex had stirred her up.

Jake grabbed his paper and stood up.

Good. She wanted him gone, needed him gone. The sooner, the better. His kindness and concern for her this morning mixed with his sexiness unnerved her. She, who always read too much into kindnesses and into making love, didn't want to soften toward him.

It wouldn't be just sex for her as it would be for him. She would weave all sorts of interlocking emotions around an act that meant next to nothing to him, and each time she went to bed with him, her feelings for him would deepen. Pretty soon she'd be thinking they had a real relationship. He would be thinking she was easy and very replaceable the minute their baby was born. She would be thinking he would become a real husband and father.

Theirs was a marriage of convenience. She was living with him for the baby's sake, so he might grow attached to it even before it was born.

For her own emotional safety, she had to keep her distance.

But could she?

Eight

By eight o'clock Monday morning, everybody who was anybody in New Orleans knew Jake Claiborne had married Alicia Butler. Their enemies, and they had legions, viewed their match with immense suspicion, just as Jake had known they would. Like vultures circling, the boldest and meanest were the first to pounce and tear off their pound of flesh.

No sooner was Jake in his building and striding down the hall toward Vanessa's office with his briefcase, than he heard his phones buzzing. Vanessa would answer one, quickly and efficiently, put the caller on hold and catch the next.

Then Jake walked into her office. Swiveling in her chair, Vanessa frowned and cupped the phone, waving him over with a swift motion.

"It's Coulter, the city manager. Line two. Third time he's called. Says it's urgent. I've got Davis on one."

Blake Davis was a heavy donor for Houses for Hurricane Victims.

"He sounds really annoyed," she said. "He isn't the only one. The phones have been ringing off the wall." She handed him a list of names and phone numbers.

Jake had expected trouble, and he was prepared to deal with it. Under no circumstances would he have even considered abandoning Alicia and their newborn baby. In time, the trouble would blow over.

"I'll take them in my office."

Without preamble Coulter told Jake he'd learned about his marriage to Miss Butler from concerned taxpayers, so he was afraid he was going to have to hire a new architect to finish the concert hall near the French Quarter.

"Sorry, Claiborne, I know she's not her father, but with her last name and his close association to you through Houses for Hurricane Victims, there'd be too much political fallout if we didn't terminate our relationship with you. We can't have any taint of scandal on this public project, especially after Katrina."

Jake picked up line one next.

"I was very disappointed by the news of your marriage to Mitchell Butler's daughter," Blake Davis said. "*Very disappointed*. Until this, I told myself you weren't involved in all that money disappearing. Needless to say, your marrying Butler's daughter would give even a naïve fool second thoughts. I'd look like an idiot if I didn't bail, damn it."

Before Jake could defend Alicia, Raymond Lewis, his top designer, barged into his office and slammed a legal document on his desk.

Jake waved the phone at Lewis, indicating he was busy. Ignoring Lewis, he spoke into the mouthpiece.

"I'm not involved with the money disappearing. Neither is my wife. She has nothing to do with any of her father's illegal activities."

"Save it for the jury. George is going to call you a little later and withdraw his support as well. Without us, HFHV is history."

"You know who you're punishing—the people who've been waiting for houses for two years."

"That should keep you up nights—not me!"

Jake sighed. He'd known when he'd married Alicia there would be fallout. What he hadn't realized was how determined he would feel about protecting Alicia.

No sooner had Davis hung up than Lewis leaned threateningly over his desk.

"What?" Jake set the receiver down. "What's wrong?"

"Your wife for starters. My letter of resignation is on your desk."

Jake glanced down, speed-reading the document. He tore it in two. "This is ridiculous."

"Not to me. When you fired all my top designers the other day, I still believed you were a man of integrity who was being unfairly judged by the media," Lewis said. "When I heard you secretly married, I wised up about you fast."

"Sorry you feel that way. I believe my wife is innocent."

"Who do you think you're kidding? Mitchell must have bought and paid for you. You're dirty, and he's threatened to spill what he knows unless you promise to take care of his little girl while he's in the slammer."

"You're very wrong. I wouldn't give that bastard the time of day."

Lewis didn't stay to argue the point. Turning on his

heel, he stalked out, banging as many doors as he could, thereby causing such a ruckus, people stopped what they were doing and stepped out of their offices to watch.

Vanessa rushed into Jake's office. "Your face is a dangerous shade of red. I'd tell you to sit down, but you're already sitting. What exactly happened in here?"

"Lewis called me a crook and quit. Unfortunately, it's becoming a familiar refrain. Not that I didn't expect something like this when word got out."

"Sorry the honeymoon had to end so fast."

What honeymoon? Jake thought bleakly.

"What do you say we get back to work—unless you're going to call me a crook and quit on me, too."

"I can't afford high-minded principles. I've got three growing sons to support. You should see my grocery bills." She smiled encouragingly.

"Glad somebody believes in my character."

She laughed. "Cheer up. When you've sunk this low, there's nowhere to go but up. Your wife's a beautiful woman. Seems kind of sweet, too. You could have done worse."

"You think so?"

She nodded.

Odd the way Vanessa's faith in Alicia eased his tension. Vanessa had excellent instincts.

"And she's a breeder. You don't always know that when you tie the knot. Your kid will be better off if the two of you figure out how to be happy together. I hope you give her a chance."

"You are not my therapist! Out!"

"That's my cue." She saluted him and made a brisk exit.

You could have done worse. And she's a breeder.

Jake leaned back in his chair and massaged his brow.

He'd been married to Alicia what, two nights? Not that he felt married exactly. No—he felt frustrated and lonely.

He never felt lonely. He liked being alone. Hell, besides having had no sex, they'd hardly spent any time together. Why was this bothering him so much when he hadn't even wanted to marry her?

Yesterday after breakfast, even though she'd locked herself in her bedroom, he hadn't wanted to leave her. To give her the run of the house, he'd stayed outside doing odd maintenance jobs like throwing out a plastic storage box full of mildewed life preservers. And all that time, he'd been wondering if she was as aware of him as he was of her.

So much for the first day of his marriage to his very sexy wife. This morning, he'd hoped that when he left for work he'd quit thinking about her. He'd been glad that, unlike her, he had somewhere to go where maybe he could get his mind off her. But even here he hadn't been able to stop thinking about her.

He'd known their marriage would cause more problems, at least in the short term. Not that it was fun to deal with the onslaught of attacks from all directions. Still, they were going to have a baby. Every time he remembered how pale and haunted Alicia had looked when she'd turned up on his doorstep with her news, he felt more determined than ever to stand by her.

When the phone rang again, he cringed. Fortunately it was only his twin brother.

"You're a lucky man," Logan said.

"Good to know somebody thinks so."

"Alicia didn't know a damn thing her father was up to."

"What makes you so sure?"

"Mitchell lied to and manipulated everybody. I know how he was with her because she and I went out…for a while. But then, you already know that," Logan trailed off awkwardly.

"Right."

Jake didn't like Logan reminding him he'd been there first with Alicia any better than he'd ever liked Logan telling him what to do or think.

"Every time I took her anywhere, people envied me," Logan said.

Jake frowned. "Well, she's married to me now."

"True. And how did that happen so fast? Last time we talked, you said she didn't want to date anybody. Then my CEO and you went to the feds and Butler really crashed in flames."

If he'd felt closer to Logan, maybe he would have told him about the pregnancy and explained the sense of responsibility he felt toward Alicia. But for a lot of years Jake had kept Logan in the dark about his life. So, for now, Jake wanted to keep it that way.

"Look, I'm sorry I didn't invite you to the wedding. If it makes you feel any better, we didn't invite anyone. Well…except for my secretary, who brought her son…but only because we needed a witnesses. Frankly, Alicia and I wanted to keep our marriage quiet as long as possible. Not easy when satellite trucks and photographers are camped on our doorstep."

"Well, the papers and Internet are full of it this morning."

"They're all damning me as a crook the equal of Butler—so you see why I wanted to keep things quiet."

"It'll blow over. Alicia's a wonderful woman."

Jake appreciated his brother's vote of confidence—not that he voiced this.

"No matter what it costs you, she'll be worth it."

Vanessa had said almost the same thing. Difficult as his relationship with Logan had been in the past, Jake respected his opinion.

"Treat her right—you hear? Someday you might have a family together."

A family. At the thought of the child that she was already secretly carrying, he felt his neck grow hot.

"Like you know everything because you're ten minutes older," Jake said.

"Being first is everything." Logan laughed.

Jake was silent.

"Well, Cici will be calling Alicia to invite you all out here to Belle Rose for dinner, so we can at least celebrate this with Grand-père, who's thrilled, by the way. The two of you could spend the weekend."

Jake's skin heated at the thought of sharing a double bed in an upstairs guest room with Alicia all night and trying to keep his hands off her.

"That's not necessary."

"Sure it is. We're family. It's about time we started acting like one."

Family. Heavy word coming from Logan, Jake thought before he said goodbye.

He began to think about his wife, wondering what Alicia could possibly be doing at home all by herself. He wanted to call her and see how she felt. He hoped she wasn't feeling nauseated.

Don't think about her. You did what she asked. You married her, didn't you? That's all you owe her.

Why didn't he feel like it was? Why did he feel... sorry for her...concerned even?

Hell. He felt a whole lot more than that. When her father had been indicted, her whole world had been destroyed. She'd lost her job and her friends in Louisiana. Maybe he was having problems himself right now, but his battles were nothing compared to hers.

Concerned about her father, she'd seemed so genuine and sweet the first night they'd met. She hadn't acted as if she had anything to hide.

If only he could stop remembering their lovemaking in such excruciating detail. She'd been so slick and warm and tight when he'd been inside her.

He wanted her again—badly.

Alicia arose from the computer, sure that if she didn't stop reading Basil Bienville's revolting blog about her marriage and her father along with the scathing comments posted by his readers, her morning sickness would return.

Those of us who've followed the scandals involving Butler Bank and Houses for Hurricane Victims shouldn't really be so amazed to learn that Alicia Butler has been living openly with Jake Claiborne. Or surprised that now we know why. According to a source close to the bride, Claiborne married the daughter of the man he turned over to the feds and publicly claims to hate Saturday evening in St. Anthony's Garden.

Why so hush-hush? Who's really responsible for the funds missing from Houses for Hurricane Victims? Does this marriage confirm what we already suspected—that Claiborne is as big a thief as Butler?

"Damn sure confirms it for me," wrote an angry reader.

If Jake hadn't married her, nobody would want to nail him to the cross.

Feeling isolated, she began to pace, wondering if there was anything lonelier than being in a house alone that wasn't one's own, especially when you were upset and needed to talk to someone—anyone. In one's own house, there were always a million little tasks to perform to distract oneself.

Not so in Jake's house—unless she read his outdoor adventure magazines or decided to answer his phone, which had rung nonstop ever since he'd left for the office. For a while she'd been too nauseated to move, so answering it had been out of the question. But her nausea seemed to be in the past now.

If in the six weeks before her marriage she'd felt as if she were dead to everybody she'd ever known, now she truly felt buried alive.

If only Carol, the one friend who'd stood by her, didn't live in London…. Damn the time difference.

Feeling the need to talk to a real friend, she sat down and dialed Carol.

Carol's voice mail picked up.

"Carol here. Sorry we're not home…."

Alicia listened to her friend's message until it ended with a beep. She almost felt like calling her back so she could hear her voice again. Instead, she left a message and then called Kimberly, who formerly had been her best friend at work. They'd gone out together to movies and concerts and for the occasional drink or dinner.

"It's me, Alicia," she said when Kim answered.

There was a telling pause. "I…I read in the paper that you got married this past weekend," Kim finally said.

"You can't believe everything you read, you know."

"I know. Still… Well, I hope you'll be very happy."

"Thanks." Alicia paused. "So, how have you been?"

"Busy. Deadlines. A couple of writers are late with their stuff. We're juggling. You know how it is."

"I've missed you so much. Missed work, too. I really need to talk to someone."

"I have missed you…. Look, Alicia, I'd love to talk. Really I would, but Sam's waving at me to get off the phone now, so I…I really do have to go."

"But, Kim, please—"

"Bye for now, Alicia. Sorry. I'll call you when I have a minute. Really I will."

Then Kim was gone. Just like Alicia's entire life was gone.

She closed her eyes and let the silence of the empty house fill her for a long moment. Deliberately trying to blank her mind, she kept them shut for ten minutes. When at last she opened them, she felt as if something inside her had shifted.

Just because things looked bad now, they didn't have to stay that way. She was pregnant. Her baby meant she had a future. Maybe a future she couldn't imagine yet, but a future. She shouldn't dwell on the past—she should make plans for the months and years ahead. Not easy when she was under siege in this house with nothing to do and her heart feeling like a heavy lump in her chest. But she could do it.

Where to start? What did people who stayed home do all day?

They had lives. They went out with their friends. They shopped. They went to their gyms. They could do these things because they still had friends and their

Get 2 Books FREE!

Silhouette® Books,
publisher of women's fiction,
presents

Silhouette®
Desire

FREE BOOKS! Use the reply card inside to get two free books!

FREE GIFTS! You'll also get two exciting surprise gifts, absolutely free!

GET 2 BOOKS

We'd like to send you two *Silhouette Desire*® novels absolutely free. Accepting them puts you under no obligation to purchase any more books.

HOW TO GET YOUR
2 FREE BOOKS AND 2 FREE GIFTS

1. Return the reply card today, and we'll send you two *Silhouette Desire* novels, absolutely free! We'll even pay the postage!

2. Accepting free books places you under no obligation to buy anything, ever. Whatever you decide, the free books and gifts are yours to keep, free!

3. We hope that after receiving your free books you'll want to remain a subscriber, but the choice is yours—to continue or cancel, any time at all!

EXTRA BONUS

You'll also get two free mystery gifts! (worth about $10)

FREE!

Return this card promptly to get
2 FREE BOOKS and 2 FREE GIFTS!

YES! Please send me 2 FREE *Silhouette® Desire*
novels, and 2 free mystery gifts as well. I understand
I am under no obligation to purchase anything, as
explained on the back of this insert.

*About how many NEW paperback fiction books have
you purchased in the past 3 months?*

❏ 0-2
E9T7

❏ 3-6
E9UK

❏ 7 or more
E9UV

225/326 SDL

FIRST NAME

LAST NAME

ADDRESS

APT.#

CITY

STATE/PROV.

ZIP/POSTAL CODE

Visit us at:
www.ReaderService.com

▶ DETACH AND MAIL CARD TODAY! ▶

(S-D-10/10)

If offer card is missing, write to The Reader Service, P.O. Box 1867, Buffalo, NY 14240-1867 or visit www.ReaderService.com

BUSINESS REPLY MAIL
FIRST-CLASS MAIL   PERMIT NO. 717   BUFFALO, NY

POSTAGE WILL BE PAID BY ADDRESSEE

THE READER SERVICE
PO BOX 1867
BUFFALO NY 14240-9952

NO POSTAGE
NECESSARY
IF MAILED
IN THE
UNITED STATES

bank accounts weren't frozen. They planned parties, fundraisers. They weren't their federally-indicted father's number one scapegoat.

Alicia walked over to a kitchen window. Lifting the drape, she stared out at the overgrown yard and beds. As a child she'd gardened with her mother. Her job and her apartment hadn't made gardening a feasible hobby. Maybe there was something outside she could do. She couldn't face days and days inside the house watching television.

Scarcely knowing what she did, she ran to her room to change. Then she let herself out the back door, banging the screen door behind her.

Curious, Gus slipped out behind her. She went into the garage and dug through drawers and shelves until she found a large straw hat, a pair of old gardening gloves that were too large and some gardening tools. Then she began to attack the beds, weeding, pruning, turning the rich, loamy soil.

Most of the yard was shaded by magnolia and oak trees. It felt good to be outdoors. Since she couldn't hear the phone, she didn't stress about the hate calls.

Once or twice she took a break and drank a tall glass of water sitting on the rocker on the veranda. The rocker made her think of the baby and how nice it might be to bring her or him out here for a feeding.

When it was time for lunch, she made herself a sandwich. After a short break, she tackled a second bed.

At least she was no longer cooped up inside. Her shoulders and lower back began to ache so much, she almost looked forward to going inside and reading an Alaska adventure story, even one that focused on bears and mosquitoes.

She was smiling at that thought when something large crashed behind her. Whirling, she stared at the hedge that lined the fence separating the front yard from the back.

"Hell," fumed a hoarse voice.

Mumbled curses were followed by more branches thrashing about and then by heavy, stumbling footsteps.

Muddy spade in hand, she stood up just as a wild-eyed, grizzled man leapt out of the azalea bushes at her.

"Well! Looky here! Caught you!" he said.

"You're not supposed to be back here, so you'd better go!"

"Or you'll what—*Mrs. Claiborne?* Scream? For your new husband? Well, he's not here, as you probably know. You won't answer your phone. You won't come to your door. How else could I talk to you?"

She didn't know whether he was dangerous or not, but her pulse was pounding in her throat as she began backing swiftly toward her kitchen door.

"Who are you?" she asked, determined to keep him talking.

"Just one of your father's investors who lost everything. Now I can't support my wife or daughter. Or put my grandchildren through college. Not that you care…"

"But I do."

"He probably spent it on you! I hoped you'd get yours when they kicked you out on the street. But you've landed on your feet, haven't you, living in this mansion with your brand-new husband! You think you're so smart you don't have to pay for what you did!"

"What do you want?"

"My money! That's what I want! Why shouldn't you pay me back what your father took?"

"Because I have no money of my own."

"Liar. Look at this house."

"Rented."

Just as he lunged toward her, the automatic gate to the driveway began to slide open. A second later Jake's big black SUV rushed down the driveway and slammed to a standstill. Jake jumped out.

It was too early for him to be home, but Alicia had never been happier to see him.

"Hey!" he yelled, shouting her name as he rushed toward her.

"Who the hell are you?" Jake demanded, stepping between Alicia and the stranger. "What the hell do you think you're doing here? Get lost. Now."

The older man stared at Jake, whose lean body looked massive and powerful even in his tailored suit. Then the man nodded slowly, as if something of Jake's meaning had penetrated.

"I'll go," he said wearily. "I'm finished here. She and her father have finished me and my whole family. You'd better be careful boy, before she finishes you, too. Or maybe you're as bad as she is."

Alicia stood behind Jake as he relocked the gate after the man had exited. Reporters eager for his story swarmed the stranger, their mikes held high.

"It's early for you to be home," Alicia said shakily to Jake.

He turned. "When I couldn't reach you by phone during lunch either on your cell or the house line, I got nervous. So I decided to drive home and check on you myself. I'm certainly glad I did."

"Me, too," she agreed weakly.

"That guy had clearly lost it."

"With good reason," she said. "He's lost all his life savings."

"Still, there's no telling what he might have done."

"I think he just wanted to vent."

"People are very angry about this. I'm going to hire you a driver, someone who'll double as your bodyguard."

"No..." She didn't want to be any more of a burden than she already was.

"So you can go out some. So you won't be totally alone here all the time."

"No!"

"I'm afraid I'm going to insist. It's for the baby's safety. Not just yours."

"Oh." His words stung a little. He didn't care about her. Still, the good part was he cared about the baby.

"So, you've been digging in the flowerbeds, I see."

"How can you tell?" she asked.

Leaning toward her, he wiped a speck of dirt off her nose and then another off her chin. Then his mouth quirked into a lopsided smile that made him too handsome to believe. "Trust me. It didn't take Sherlock Holmes."

"I was very scared before you came," she said, her voice breaking in heartfelt gratitude.

"And I felt crazier and crazier at the office when you didn't answer." He caught himself. Clearly he felt awkward about revealing his concern. "Well, speaking of the office, I'd better get back to work."

"Yes. Sorry to be such a bother. I'll try to be better behaved."

He smiled. "Then promise me you won't go into the

backyard alone until I find someone to see after you. And why don't you get a new cell phone number so I can reach you."

Feeling pleased that he was so protective, and a little shy, she nodded.

When he left, she stood at a front window and watched him drive away. Long after he'd disappeared she continued to stare at the lengthy shadows beneath the trees across the street.

When she finally turned back to face the empty house, she didn't feel quite as lonely as she had before. Her heart felt lighter, her mood brighter. She actually looked forward to making plans for the future and shopping for the baby with a driver.

Jake had come home because of her.

He'd protected her and the baby.

For no reason at all she kept remembering the way he'd smiled so tenderly when he'd wiped the dirt off her nose.

He didn't really care. Not about her.

Still…it felt nice to pretend that he might.

Nine

The more Alicia tried to ignore Jake, the more fascinated by him she grew.

She knew that there were no photographs or personal memorabilia in his house. It was as if he wanted no link to his past. Why? Had he had a difficult past too?

She knew the exact hour he left for work. Seven-thirty. On the dot.

She knew the exact hour he came home. Six-thirty.

She knew that he had trouble sleeping, that he often paced at night, pausing at her door. The knob would turn and she would sit up, listening in the dark, charged with the hope and fear that he might open it.

She knew what he ate for dinner—fast food because she found the wadded wrappers and boxes in the trash. Pizza mostly. Way too much pizza.

It's none of your business that he never eats vegetables.

A real wife would at least cook healthier choices for him. But it was dangerous to even think she might ever be that woman.

Too often Alicia thought about Jake rescuing her from that man in the garden. It seemed uncanny that he'd known just when to come home. It was as if he were tuned into her in a psychic way.

When she relived that scene, she wished she'd kissed him.

Stupid. A kiss wouldn't change anything. She was the woman he'd married reluctantly and kept hidden away from his business associates, friends and family; the woman he chose never to be seen with in public.

After two whole weeks of living such separate lives, Alicia felt like she was going mad. She longed to eat with him, to talk to him—to know him better, to know why he looked so increasingly tense.

"He sounds nicer than I pictured him," Carol said during one of their morning chats as Alicia prepared a beef stew for her dinner. "And his photographs on the Web are absolutely hunky."

Tell me about it.

"Coming home like that…at just the right moment when that man was in your backyard, it's no wonder…"

"No wonder what?"

"No wonder that you're having these fantasies and starting to like him."

Grrrrr. "I am not having fantasies or starting to like him," she grumbled, hating that she was so easy to read even over an overseas phone call.

"If you say so, love."

For some reason Alicia didn't snap back with a sassy retort.

Carol had started calling her a couple of times a week after she'd heard Alicia's message when Alicia had phoned her when she'd been so depressed.

"You should never have stayed in Louisiana," Carol said. "You should have come to London and taken that job I found you."

"I know. Part of me agrees. But I felt I had to give him a chance…for the baby's sake… Being here, at least, means the baby is part of his life."

"Well, that was very generous of you, under the circumstances."

"I know what it feels like to be without a parent. Really without any parents. What if I died, and the baby ended up with strangers?"

"Still, I can't help thinking you would have been better off to have gotten clean away from that whole mess, started over here in the U.K., you know what I mean. Nobody's ever heard of Dear Old Daddy being accused of anything over here."

"Sounds lovely. Jake thinks Daddy's a criminal, and since he sees me solely as Daddy's daughter, well…he probably thinks I'm guilty, too."

"Are you sure about that?"

"Well, he's said it often enough."

He hadn't said it lately. But that was only because they barely spoke.

"Well, after you have the baby and the baby's old enough, I'll whisk you and the baby over here and take care of you. I have so many friends, many of them men, and they'll all adore you. You'll forget Jake in no time. You'll meet a handsome Brit, fall madly in love and live happily ever after."

Carol's supportive attitude warmed her. But the

thought of leaving Jake and then their child growing up far from its father did not.

That evening when Jake came home early, she was still out in the backyard digging. Victor, her bodyguard/ chauffeur, had helped her buy a crib for the nursery, more azaleas and a birdcage to house an injured mourning dove she'd rescued on the back veranda as well as several bird feeders. Victor had set up the birdcage, the crib and the feeders, but she hadn't yet finished preparing the soil to plant the azaleas. She hadn't come inside and eaten the beef stew she'd cooked. She was tired but eager to finish what she'd started.

Suddenly Jake was just there, towering behind her as he watched her attack his flowerbed like a dog burying a treasured bone. Since she didn't know he was there, she slung a shovel load of dirt onto his expensive Italian loafer.

"Hey," he said, chuckling as he shook his foot. "Aren't you getting a little carried away? If you don't stop that we'll have to shower together."

She whirled. His eyes were shadowed despite his amusement. He looked exhausted, both physically and mentally.

But when their glances touched, he smiled, that quick, sexy flash of straight white teeth that always made her stomach feel hollow…but in that good way. She felt a zing.

Before she thought, she smiled right back at him. The thought of showering with him held way too much appeal.

He knelt and cupped her elbow lightly. "I'll bet that'll wait until tomorrow. You don't want to overtire yourself."

Her breath caught. "What are you doing home this early?"

"I brought some work home."

"Oh." She turned back to the flowerbed and continued to dig, but not quite so vigorously as before. She was too aware of the electric heat of his touch, of his nearness, of the desire to be held closely in his arms.

"You know, I think there are fewer trucks outside. Maybe the media's interest in us is lessening just a bit."

"Hope so."

He let her go and stood up. "I met Victor out front. Told him he could go home for the day, that I'd see about you this afternoon."

She was too conscious of his long shadow falling across her. She wished he'd kneel again and touch her. Just her elbow would be enough.

Instead he took a step backward. He'd been being polite, that was all.

"Well, I guess I'll go inside and get to work," he said after watching her for a while longer.

No doubt he'd quickly vanish upstairs and lock her out of his office. Gus would probably follow him as he usually did, and she would be as lonely as she was every night. Only lonelier because she'd feel left out after Jake had been so nice.

That cat of hers was incorrigible. He would never stay in her room once Jake came home. If she tried to force him, he would go to the door and yowl and paw until she let him out. If she ever felt lonely enough to crack her door to see what was going on in the rest of the house, she would sometimes hear violent blasts of sound from Jake's television set upstairs and imagine her cat napping serenely at Jake's feet while macho actors gunned each other down.

If she went into the kitchen to find a snack, she would discover Jake's fast-food wrappers in the garbage and guilt about his bad diet would gnaw even as she reminded herself what he wanted was no wife at all.

When the screen door banged behind him, she raced after him, slowing her pace when she neared the kitchen because she did not want him to think her in a mad hurry to catch up to him, although she was.

"Smells good," he said, sounding almost wistful when she walked into the kitchen.

"Beef stew. Nothing fancy."

"Reminds me that I was so tired and ready to get home I forgot to stop and get anything to eat tonight. Pizza every night gets old."

Was that a hint? "Would you like some stew? There's enough for two."

"I think I would…if you don't mind. Why don't you wash up while I set the table?"

Did that mean he was calling a truce?

"Okay. I'll just be a second," she whispered in a voice that was much too breathy and eager.

He grinned broadly. "I think it may take you longer than that."

"Do I look that horrible?"

"Loaded question, *cher*. But no, you don't look horrible. You look cute that way."

What way? She ran to her bedroom, only to let out a little shriek and stomp her feet when she saw her filthy reflection in the mirror. Did she only imagine his chuckle? Flecks of black dirt spotted her face, shirt and shorts and greased her arms.

She kicked off her muddy shoes and shed her grimy

clothes. Showering quickly, she tied her hair in a red ribbon and put on a pair of red capris and a white shirt. Then she slipped on gold bangles and a pair of gold sandals. The last thing she did was dab her wrists with perfume.

When she returned to the kitchen the flash of heat in Jake's blue eyes and his crooked grin told her that she looked presentable.

He'd poured himself a glass of wine and her a glass of sparkling water garnished with a slice of lime. He'd put on music and had set the table for two in the dining room. A contented Gus lay in the middle of the kitchen, his tail lazily thumping the tile as he waited for the stew to come out of the oven. She knew that behind her back, Jake fed Gus table scraps. The scene felt too domestic and comfortable and was much too close to her dream of a fantasy marriage with a man she loved.

"So, how was your day?" he asked, his interested gaze sweeping her and making her feel hot and strange.

"Same as always," she replied, her tone clipped as she sipped her icy water and fought to shore up her defenses.

"The yard's looking good."

"At least it's given me something to do. And I feel happy outside. And your day?"

"Still putting out fires that have to do with my association with your father and now my marriage to you," he said coolly. "Today was particularly bad. The entire Houses for Hurricane Victims board dropped by and demanded my resignation. After that meeting, I decided to come home."

"I'm sorry."

"It was a cause close to my heart...so, bad subject. What do you say we change it?"

"What would you prefer to talk about?"

"You," he said.

"We already did that. The first night we met when I stupidly confided my entire life story to you...before I knew who you really were and what you were about to do to my father. Remember?"

Fire flashed in his eyes and she regretted goading him.

"All right, then. You choose what we talk about," he said.

"You."

"Boring subject."

"Maybe to you."

"All right. What do you want to know?"

"Why were you estranged from your family for nine years?"

He flinched involuntarily, and just for an instant she thought she saw pain shadow his eyes. Then his features hardened into that neutral mask that was all too familiar. It was his habit to shut people out, to keep them at a distance.

"My brother took the woman I'd loved all my life away from me, so I left," he said, so bitterly she felt as if a fist had grabbed her heart and squeezed hard.

Ask a tough question, you get a tough answer.

"You mean Cici?" she whispered.

"Do we have to talk about this?" He yanked at the knot of his silk tie as if his collar had suddenly tightened to the point it was choking him. Then he unbuttoned the top two buttons of his shirt.

At the strip of dark hair now visible at the base of his throat, she sucked in her breath.

"Was it Cici?" she said.

"Yes," he said. *"Cici.* He took her and discarded her

to save me, he said. He broke her heart and married a wealthy, suitable girl."

Savagely he slung his tie across a kitchen chair. "I found that hard to forgive."

Because his heart, the heart he guarded so closely, had been shattered.

"What happened to Logan's first wife?"

"She died."

"And you... Are you still in love with Cici?" She hated the way her husky voice was suddenly quivering.

"No. But that doesn't mean I trust my brother."

Maybe he wasn't being entirely honest about no longer loving Cici. Alicia knew she shouldn't care. Then why did she feel as if that awful fist around her heart had tightened?

"But you came back," she whispered, her tone barely audible.

"This is my home. When Katrina struck, and so many people needed houses and help of the most basic kind, I had the right skills to make a difference. I felt compelled to return. Though I wasn't ready to connect with a family I believed to be ruthlessly materialistic and cruel. Do you understand why I had at least some sympathy for your problems with your father that night? But then, Hayes Daniels hadn't filled me in on the whole story yet."

Jake's eyes were blazing suddenly.

"I'll get the stew," she said quietly, not wanting to push him—or herself—any closer to such dangerous subjects. Not that she could forget that he'd made a play for her that first night only after Cici had gone after Logan.

"Why don't we eat out on the back veranda? I need some fresh air," he said.

"Okay," she agreed.

In silence he moved the place settings to the table outside while she got their dinner ready to serve. He did not look at her or speak to her again as they spooned food onto their plates and carried them along with their drinks outside.

Despite the humidity it was a lovely evening with voluminous, pink thunderheads looming in the west. Oblivious to the distant storms, birds sang in the trees as they settled down for the night. She could hear a child playing with a barking dog in a nearby yard. But most of all she was conscious of Jake sitting across the table from her. He looked tall and dark, smoldering even, as the delicious scent of his aftershave wafted toward her disturbingly.

For a while he ate in brooding silence, his spoon clinking against his bowl. And all the while as she started at every clink, she felt like she was holding her breath.

One question thrummed in her primitive, female brain—was he still in love with Cici? He'd said he wasn't. Why couldn't she just take him at his word?

"So, where did you go?" Alicia finally said, persisting despite the agony in her heart.

He looked up, his gaze so intense she had to inhale a steadying breath.

"What?"

"When you left Louisiana all those years ago. Where did you go? What did you do?"

"You don't give up easily, do you?"

"I was an editor. It goes with the territory."

Much to her surprise he unleashed a wary grin. "Like you said, you told me everything *that* first night…."

"Except the embarrassing location of my heart-shaped birthmark."

When his grin grew wicked and his gaze drifted to her left breast and lingered, heat suffused her throat and spread upward to her cheeks. She could have kicked herself for that slip.

"I found that out for myself, didn't I? A most delightful discovery, by the way. But I'm sure I told you that when I made love to you."

His last sentence seemed to hang in the air. The quick, volcanic burst of fire that washed through her had nothing to do with the summer evening and everything to do with the memory of his sensual mouth nibbling her breasts and sucking her nipples, of his large male body pressing close.

Wishing with all her heart that she could erase the vision of his virile mating, she sat up taller. "You were about to tell me where you went," she reminded him.

"Where all young American men with something to prove have always gone traditionally. Out West. To Utah, Arizona, Colorado, New Mexico…California. And then to Alaska. I traveled with a friend…Paul…for a while." His voice darkened. "We hiked, kayaked, camped out, rock climbed, did manual labor to pay our way."

"Where's Paul now?"

"He died. Because of a damn fool idea of mine to go rock climbing. He fell."

He paused, and she was stunned at the sudden pain that welled up in his eyes, which were now dark blue pools.

"I'm so sorry," she said.

"It was a long time ago. I'm over it." His expression was blank and cold.

Was he? Was he over Cici as well? Guilt and love

could have very long tails. "Still, it's too bad that he…" Her voice was soft, gentle, consoling.

"His death taught me life is too short to waste. So I got a grip on my anger and pulled myself together. I went back to school. I found that I liked building things. I think I became an architect because I envisioned myself building houses that would be homes for happy couples. Not that I know anything about being part of a happy family. When I graduated I went to work, and I got lucky. Or maybe luck comes to the driven. All I know is that as long as I was working, I was fairly happy for a while, at least professionally. Then one day my luck ran out."

"When was that?"

"The day I nominated your father to the board of Houses for Hurricane Victims. The only reason he was unanimously elected was because of my recommendation."

The sudden harshness in his voice and eyes brought her up short. Maybe because she hadn't seen the blow coming, she felt more vulnerable than usual. It hurt more. It was as if he'd reached across the table and struck her.

"He'll always be between us, won't he? You'll always hate me for what you think he did." Maybe Cici would be between them, too, for that matter. But she didn't dare throw Cici at him. What if he told her flat out he loved Cici?

"He did it. That's not even in question," Jake said.

She shut her eyes, hating herself for doubting her father. "So, you'll never in a thousand years be able to forgive me for being the daughter of the man you believe cost you so much."

With a sharp intake of breath, he clenched his hands.

"Am I right?" she demanded.

He glanced angrily away from her toward the yard.

"You won't," she said. "I accept that. Look, I…I think I made a mistake to eat with you," she said. "I don't know why I ever thought you and I could have a civil conversation…even for one meal. I'll eat later. By myself." She stood up to go.

He rushed to his feet, too. "The hell you will."

His eyes were so fierce her chest tightened, and suddenly she could barely breathe.

How could this happen? One minute they'd been eating dinner, talking. Then their conversation had veered into forbidden territory. Now suddenly she felt herself caught in a swirling conflagration of conflicting, hot-blooded emotions.

"I don't understand what you want with me," she whispered. "You've ignored me ever since we married and now…"

"I made it clear from the first I want you in my bed."

"And I told you why that's not possible. Good night, Jake."

"Like hell," he muttered.

She intended to whip past him and head inside to safety, but he was faster. He caught up to her in a single stride. Clamping his strong hand around her upper arm, he yanked her against his hard body.

When she was too stunned to fight him, he swung her even tighter against his body and then walked her backward until they stood, his body flattening her breasts and pressing her spine against the wall of his house.

The mask was gone. His blue eyes blazed. "For days I've wanted to touch you and hold you. God, you feel good."

Oh, so did he. She felt like she was melting into him, every cell in her body dissolving and flowing into his.

"I don't want to want you, but I do. More and more. Every day," he said.

"You do?"

"Then I think about what your father did and feel torn."

She felt torn about her father, too. Growing up, she'd always known he was ruthlessly ambitious. In business it was so easy for those in power to ride roughshod over the little people. Of late, it was increasingly difficult for her to believe that her father was innocent, and yet she felt deeply conflicted about that. She wanted to stand by him.

"You're driving me crazy," Jake said. "There's you and the baby on one side, and him and what happened, what's still happening, on the other. I feel like I'm living in hell."

"Me, too."

"Time to end it," he whispered. His hand cupped her chin. For a long moment, his eyes searched hers as if asking her for something. Then his lips took hers in a searing kiss.

"Don't," she pleaded, tearing her mouth free.

"We're getting a divorce eventually, remember? I won't complicate this horrible mess further."

"Shut up," he said, his voice hoarse. Then his mouth came down on hers again, claiming her in a raw act of possession while his hands and body crushed her closer.

After he explored the sweet wetness of her mouth

thoroughly, warmth from his lips and tongue slowly stole through her body, making her ache for more. After feeling so alone all day, indeed for weeks, it felt thrillingly wonderful to be held and kissed with such wild abandon by a man so determined to control his emotions.

Deep down she had wanted this, too. Wanted him. Obsessed about this. Most of all she wanted to be wanted this much. When she felt his aroused manhood pushing against her thighs, his intense physical need was a healing balm to the deep psychological wound that her father's indifference had inflicted. At least Jake wasn't indifferent. She wanted to be loved so much. To be wanted…even just for this.

When the thrusts of Jake's tongue took on a sexual rhythm, instead of protesting, her hands circled his neck. Her body tingling all the ways to her toes, she clung to him and sighed. She was on the verge of surrendering everything to him when she heard the sound of glass shattering at the front of the house. People in the front yard began to shout and curse.

Panting hard, furious, he jerked free of her. "Damn it, what's going on now?"

"Sounds like another brick through your window."

His eyes were wild as he gently smoothed her hair. "Don't you move a single inch, sweetheart. I'm coming right back to finish what we've started."

Then he was gone.

Like a sick, love-struck fool she remained paralyzed for long minutes, her blood humming. But when he didn't come back, and her pulse slowed, her power to reason gradually returned.

Knowing all that stood between them, she could not

let her passions rule her. She would not surrender so easily.

Very deliberately she walked into the house and down the hall to her bedroom.

Ten

When Jake strode back inside the front door, he was still on fire for Alicia. She wasn't where he'd left her and she searched the house.

Breathing hard, he returned to the nursery and stood in the doorway for a long moment. Every night lately, after the constant attacks at work, he'd come here and had found comfort in this room with the soft yellow quilts and valences with blue bunnies on them. He would imagine her holding their baby, playing with it, reading to it. Imagine himself joining in, imagine them down on their knees, playing with their baby together.

He would put his arm around her and her dark eyes would shine with shared tenderness. Their baby would not want its parents to hate each other or live apart from each other. Surely she would see that.

Was he a fool to imagine such scenes? Strangely, he had begun to look forward to coming home at night just to see what else she'd done in here. He'd begun to wish she wanted to spend time with him, to wish he'd treated her differently right from the first. He hated how he'd prejudged her, blaming her for every crime her father had committed. He'd begun to wonder if he'd been wrong.

In two short weeks she'd made it a real nursery. His child had become more real to him and infinitely precious.

Even though adjusting to having her as his wife was still difficult for him and very costly professionally, he knew he'd get through this. Every evening he looked forward to leaving the office and opening this door. It was like stepping into an entirely new world, one that was full of possibility…and hope.

Was it ridiculous to dream of such a future with her when there was so much bad blood between them?

Quietly he left the nursery. Her bedroom door was closed, but the sliver brightness that lit its bottom made him suspect she was probably inside hiding from him.

Well, after the stunt he'd pulled, he damn sure had it coming. Fisting his hand, he raised it to her door. Instead of knocking, he froze as he often did in the dead of the night. The last thing he wanted to do was to scare her again.

"Alicia?" he whispered.

Something rustled on the other side of the door. Then, to his amazement, the door opened, if just a crack. Had she been waiting for him all the time?

He couldn't see that much of her, but with her big brown eyes glimmering up at him in confusion while her dark hair fell in tangles about her throat, she was too sexy for words. It didn't hurt that her red lips were still moist and swollen from being so thoroughly kissed.

If ever a woman looked like she needed more kissing, it was Alicia.

The permanent knot in his throat tightened and his blood began to burn again. His groin ached.

How could he live in the same house with her another night if he didn't sleep with her? He clenched his hands and struggled to control his harsh breathing.

"I regret the caveman tactics," he heard himself mutter hoarsely.

"I understand," she said. Her soft voice cut his heart like sharp glass. "You're forgiven."

She didn't sound like she was over their encounter any more than he was, but he didn't call her on it.

"That's very generous of you," he said.

"So, what was all the excitement out front about?"

At least she hadn't shut her door in his face.

"The usual. Another angry investor got drunk and threw a rock through our window."

"Same window?"

"Afraid so. Luckily a couple of the reporters made themselves useful and tackled him. I told the self-righteous vandal to go home and sleep it off. Then they all wanted to interview me."

"This is all my fault."

"Don't…. He's gone for now. I'm on my way out to the garage to get a board and some nails to cover the window."

"I'll help you with that if you want," she said, almost eagerly. He felt an answering excitement because her offer pleased him far too much.

He nodded.

"I'll just get my shoes," she said.

He liked hearing her soft-soled footsteps trailing behind him all the way out to the garage. Despite the reporters taking pictures and the hecklers yelling at them from the front yard, he enjoyed her carrying the nails for him and holding the board steady while he nailed it.

"I'll call someone tomorrow to repair it," he said when he was through hammering and they were safely back inside the house.

"No, let me. I'm home all day. It's the least I can do."

She was so sweet and so eager to please. Surely that was a good sign. "Okay. Thank you."

She turned to go. He ached to seize her and kiss her again. But even though his heart pounded violently, he didn't.

As her slim, solitary figure moved gracefully down the hall, he stood transfixed watching the gentle sway of her hips. Dear God... The memory of their recent kiss had him so hot with desire to hold her and kiss her again that he couldn't resist calling after her.

"Alicia—" He caught himself then, afraid she'd see or hear something that would make her know how acute his need was.

She pivoted sharply. Light from the chandelier in the dining room slanted across her long neck. Her gaze was sharp, almost piercing. Why did she have to be so damned beautiful?

Too beautiful to hate.

With a start he began to dwell on the reality that he didn't dislike her and that maybe he never had. Not even from the first. His wanting her wasn't just lust anymore—if it ever had been. Then what was it?

What was going on here? What was happening to him?

He had thought he loved Cici, but what he felt now for Alicia was even more powerful.

He hadn't fought for Cici. Even though Alicia was Butler's daughter, he knew that if any man threatened her, he'd give his life to protect her.

He would never have chosen Alicia as his wife, but now that she was, he couldn't imagine anyone else ever taking her place any more than he could imagine ever wanting to let her go. Why had he ever thought he could easily divorce her?

Maybe he would just have to accept that there were some things between a man and woman that couldn't be explained. He didn't know why or when she'd come to matter to him so much. But matter she did—and more every day.

The terms of his marriage which included never touching her again and divorcing her as soon as possible now seemed hellish and impossible.

"Alicia…" His voice broke.

"Yes, Jake," she said in that soft honeyed tone that could turn him to mush.

"I was thinking…that maybe…I mean if you want to…" He sounded worse than a horny teenager awkwardly asking a girl he had a crush on out for the first time. "I mean maybe I could take you out to dinner… tomorrow night."

Her eyes shone for a moment. "That's not necessary, Jake. I've cost you as much as you've cost me."

"I know it's not necessary. That's not the point. I want things to be different between us. Better. I mean, hell, we're going to have a baby together. Maybe we should try to at least be cordial to each other. Friends?"

He could never be friends with her.

"All right then," she agreed. "Dinner."

"I'll look forward to it."

He held his breath, willing her to walk into his arms.

Instead, she shyly lowered her eyes, turned on her slender heel and vanished, leaving him staring after her. Marriage, he thought bitterly as he stood in the gloom, had become his own peculiar brand of hell.

"Goodbye, Jake," Alicia said as she followed him him as he went out the back door.

Walking with him to his car every morning when he left for his office had become a pleasant routine this past month.

He turned around and waited for her. His red tie slanted across his broad chest at a cockeyed angle. If she had been his real wife, she would have reached up and straightened it. Maybe she would have kissed him on his tanned cheek and then whispered in his ear not to forget that today was her birthday.

He would ask her what she wanted and she would either tell him or tease him, saying she wanted him to surprise her.

Instead she said, "Your tie is crooked." After a quick glance at her, he said a gruff "thanks" and straightened it.

"Is it all right now?" he asked with a smile.

A wealth of emotions hung in the air as their eyes touched briefly.

She was standing on the exact spot on the veranda where he'd seized her and kissed her a month ago.

She sighed. "Perfect."

Although they were on much friendlier terms, she hadn't told him today was her special day. If he didn't know, how could he disappoint her?

Not that she hadn't wanted to tell him. She'd held back mainly because her father had always forgotten or ignored her birthdays, and she didn't want to risk Jake being indifferent, too.

"Who has the time for birthdays?" her father had said on more than one occasion when she'd dared complain.

Yes, a whole month had passed since Jake had kissed her against her will right here and then had apologized by taking her out to eat the next evening to an elegant meal at her favorite French restaurant in the Quarter. That night he'd gone overboard being nice and polite to her, repeating that he'd desired a less hostile relationship with the future mother of his child.

"But could you ever really forgive me?" she'd asked as the candle on their table had lit the right side of his face and eyes with golden light.

"Could you forgive me for blowing the whistle on your father? For conspiring with my brother's CEO, Hayes Daniels, to set him up for prison?" he'd countered.

Neither had said they could. Even so, ever since he'd been exceptionally deferential toward her. She now looked forward to being with him and dreaded her evenings alone when he was away on one of his frequent business trips to Orlando.

In a state of wistful longing, she stood on the veranda until the gates closed and his SUV disappeared from view. When the phone began to ring, she ran back inside the kitchen and then stopped short when she saw the familiar name blazing on the caller ID.

She picked it up anyway. "Hello, Daddy."

"Happy birthday, pumpkin," he said, stunning her into silence.

"You remembered," she finally whispered, pleased in spite of herself. Maybe he was adjusting to her marriage after all.

"I'd invite you to lunch or something…take you shopping…but…but you understand why that's not possible."

Since he didn't mention he was under house arrest, neither did she. "I know. And that's okay. I mean…it's not okay…but—"

He interrupted her. "I know what you mean. I'd like to see you. I've missed you. We could still have lunch, if you brought a pizza or hamburgers over here…or carry-out from any restaurant you'd like."

"I…I'm afraid I can't come," she said. Her promise to Jake stood between them.

"Oh." His voice sounded dead and lost. "Is it because of him?"

"Yes," she admitted. "He doesn't think I should see you. I'm sorry."

"It's okay."

But it wasn't. He sounded so down. And who could blame him?

"Are you all right?" she asked.

"No. It's your birthday…and God knows I've missed enough of your birthdays in my time. Your mother always made such a fuss—over both of us. I missed the fuss as much as you did. I thought this year I might make it up to you."

"I'll be there within the hour," she promised. He sounded so bleak. But as she held the phone so tightly her fingers ached she wondered how she'd ever pull a stunt like this off without Jake finding out.

"Do you need anything?" she asked.

"Razors. Toothpaste. Sugarless gum."

He sounded so diminished. How could she possibly say no?

* * *

"I feel like a spy," Alicia said as she slipped across her father's threshold and he quickly shut the door behind her.

She pulled her scarves and sunglasses off and shook out her hair. When she handed her father a sack containing the items he'd requested, his hard gaze swept her. A guard slipped forward to inspect what she'd brought. Nodding, the guard backed away.

"Marriage doesn't suit you. You look exhausted."

In the past he'd rarely commented on her appearance if it didn't involve the public; he'd always been too self-involved.

She could have said he looked tired, too, because he did, worrisomely so. The strong and powerful-looking father she'd admired and feared was gone. The man before her had dark rings around his eyes and was so shrunken in stature she was now several inches taller than he was. His hair was snow-white.

"Daddy, do we have to quarrel? Today?"

"I suppose not…since it's your birthday," he said.

She didn't have much time to be with him. She'd told Victor she wanted to shop for the nursery in the French Quarter. Then she'd lost him and had taken a cab to her father's mansion across town. She doubted her sunglasses and scarves had concealed her identity from the single reporter camped outside her father's home.

She felt guilty about giving Victor the slip and deceiving Jake, and she needed to get back to the French Quarter to find Victor within the hour. Otherwise he wouldn't grow alarmed and alert Jake. If Jake found out she'd gone off on her own, he'd probably fire Victor.

"How could you betray me by marrying Claiborne?" her father asked.

"You never give up," she said.

"Does he?"

"Look, I didn't exactly want to marry him, okay?" She stopped herself. The last thing she wanted was to discuss Jake or her pregnancy.

"Well, at least you haven't totally lost your senses. Why did you do it then? How'd he make you? What does he have on you?"

"Let's not talk about Jake or why I married him. It's not a good subject for us."

"To say the least."

After a brief pause she changed tacks. "I brought pizza. Pepperoni. Your favorite." It was Jake's favorite, too, but, of course, she couldn't say that.

He gave the pizza box a long look and then shrugged before leading her into the dining room away from the guard, who remained in the living room. She set the table and her father ate in gloomy silence while she sipped tea.

His tomblike house was a whole lot quieter and lonelier than it used to be. He'd always been a man of action who worked all day and went out all night. When he'd been home, phones had rung constantly. How did he stand the silence and inactivity?

"You're not eating?" he asked after a while.

"I'll eat later." She didn't tell him that pizza upset her stomach if she ate it this early in the day. If she told him she sometimes suffered from nausea in the mornings, he'd put two and two together.

"I have a present for you," her father said after his cup of coffee.

"There's no need…really…."

Glancing toward the living room where the guard was on his cell phone, he got up and pulled a black ebony box that she recognized as her mother's out of a drawer and handed it to her.

Upon opening the lacquered box, she gasped. With shaking fingers she lifted the sparkling diamond pin in the shape of a starfish from the bed of black velvet. Smiling at him, she caressed each point of the star with a fingertip, just to make sure they were all there.

"Your mother wore it every day," he said, his deep voice rough behind her.

"I know."

"It was her mother's and maybe her mother's before her I think."

Sudden tears pricked Alicia's lashes but she wiped them away. She remembered too well how the pin used to flash on her dear mother's collar. Alicia had always loved this piece of jewelry. She remembered sneaking into her mother's room sometimes when she'd played dressup and opening the lacquered box just to gaze at it and count the points of the star.

"No, it's too valuable," she said, replacing the pin in the box and handing it to him. "Besides, the authorities said they own everything now."

"Forget them." He glanced toward the guard, who was still on his phone. "They'd take everything if we let them. This'll be our little secret. Like I said, this was your grandmother's before it was your mother's. I know how much you loved your mother. I loved her, too. Pumpkin, one reason I wasn't around much after she was gone was because you reminded me too much of her."

"Oh?" Was that really true? she wondered.

"Also, I told myself that I was making all that money for you."

"Daddy, I can't take it."

"She would have wanted you to have it. Besides, it's your birthday. If I end up in prison, it may be the last present I can ever give you on your birthday."

"Don't say that."

"Well, like I said, I've missed too many of your birthdays. I didn't want to ignore this one…because it could be my last chance…"

"Daddy, that's really so sweet, but if I took it, it might get you into more trouble."

"Okay. I understand." Closing the box, he replaced it in the drawer.

He looked so disappointed she got up and put her arms around him. "But Daddy, thank you so much for thinking of me!"

He stiffened and refused to look at her, since she wasn't doing what he wanted.

Touching his cheek, she said, "Maybe you won't go to prison. Maybe you'll be exonerated."

"Dream on," he said wearily. "A lot of liars like your husband, who will stop at nothing, are conspiring to frame me."

Hesitantly she said, "Jake told me about the money missing from Houses for Hurricane Victims. He said you were in charge of investing those funds. If you didn't take that money, then surely you must have an idea of who did."

"He would say that, of course! And you're always so gullible, you believed him." Letting her go, he stared at her as if she had become someone he didn't really know. "He's getting to you, isn't he? Turning you against me?"

"Did you take that money, Daddy? From the charity? From the bank?"

He turned away. "Who do you think you are—to

accuse me? You're married to the real crook. When he's through with you, he'll toss you out like so much garbage."

"You didn't answer my question."

"Because I never thought I'd live to see the day when a daughter of mine would ask me such a thing. *You know me*."

"Do I?"

Her father grew morose and silent. After sitting with him for ten more minutes and trying in vain to make small talk, she finally gave up and told him she had to go. He nodded indifferently.

The guard checked her purse and shopping bags again at the door, but then at the last minute her father said something, so she went back to give him a goodbye hug. Throwing up his hands to ward off her embrace, he sent her purse and bags flying, spilling their contents under his couch and easy chair.

"Sorry," he muttered as he knelt to retrieve her things.

"I'll do it," she whispered.

"No! Stay where you are," he thundered as he pulled a lipstick out from under a chair. "You caused enough trouble—by marrying Jake Claiborne."

When her father stood up, he was panting hard. He slammed the purse and bags into her hands.

"Goodbye," she whispered.

Turning away, he slumped back in his chair. She took a taxi back to the Quarter, where she found Victor. Later when she was safely back home, she went to her desk, intending to file the receipts for the things she'd bought for the nursery. But when she opened her shopping bags to look for the receipts, she found the lacquered box her father had tried to give her. When she lifted the lid, dazzling sparks of light glinted from her mother's lovely pin.

"Oh, no!"

She sagged against her chair, her heart pounding. Why did her father have to be so hardheaded? Why couldn't he just once take no for an answer? He was under house arrest. Didn't he realize how serious that was? Even if this pin had belonged to her mother, he should abide by the terms of his arrest.

She loved the pin, and he knew it. He'd thought she should have it for her birthday, so he'd found a way to slip it into a bag after the guard had checked them. If she took the pin back, she would get him into even worse trouble. A second trip would risk involving Jake again.

Torn, she closed the box and stared at it for what seemed an eternity. After a long while she got up, carried it to her bedroom and slid it under her mattress. Later she would figure out what to do about the pin.

Right now she wanted to concentrate on happier things…like Jake and her baby. Gathering her shopping bags, she hurried to the nursery and began putting away the things she'd bought for the baby.

Eleven

Alicia was straightening up the nursery when the phone rang.

Had the authorities missed her mother's pin so soon?

Or was it Jake calling to ask about her day? How could she talk to him without mentioning her visit to her father and the pin, which were so heavy on her mind? She would—she had to.

Then, hoping the caller actually was her husband, she ran out into the hall to catch the phone.

"Alicia?" The lilting, feminine voice was vaguely familiar, yet she couldn't place it.

"Yes."

"It's Cici! Logan's wife. I don't know if you remember me. We met at Pierre's birthday party."

As if she could ever forget her dancing so wildly with

Logan, who'd been her date, or anything else about *that* night.

"I remember," she said.

Even though he said he was over her, Alicia felt too unsure of their relationship to feel totally secure around a woman he'd once been involved with. She wished she could stop remembering how erotically Cici had danced with Logan.

"Logan and I want to invite you and Jake to dinner. Here at Belle Rose with Pierre."

"Oh? How nice."

Sounding sincerely friendly, Cici rushed on, giving her possible dates, saying they had some happy news too, suggesting a Friday or a Saturday so they could stay over and avoid a late night drive back to New Orleans.

"I'll talk to Jake and get back to you later today."

"That would be lovely. We can't wait to see you both and congratulate you. We're very happy you're family."

"Thank you."

She asked after Pierre. After a brief conversation, they hung up.

Alicia felt more uncertain than ever as she held the phone. The pin hidden under her mattress worried her, as did Cici's warmth and eagerness to entertain them and celebrate their marriage. What if seeing Logan and Cici together made Jake focus on his past love?

Still she should call Jake and tell him about the invitation. No. She would go to his office. Better to see his face when she told him Cici had called.

Jake was thumbing through an annual report on a project in Orlando while deep in conversation with his head man on that venture when Vanessa suddenly burst into his office. Expecting bad news, he stared up at her.

"Sorry to be a bother, but your wife is here, sir." Her voice was tight and low. "She's been here awhile and I have to tell you—she's upsetting the natives. The sooner you see her, the better."

Jake didn't say a word; he was too surprised. Quickly he terminated his call and rushed out to Vanessa's office.

"I hope you're not too busy," Alicia began as she stood up, glancing uncertainly at Vanessa before she looked at him. "Some of your employees weren't happy to see me in the elevator."

"I'm sorry if my people were rude. It's as much my fault as yours that tensions have been running so high around here of late. As far as I'm concerned, this is a pleasant surprise." Frowning at his secretary, who was watching them with excessive interest, he took his wife's arm and led her into his office. "We'd like coffee, if that's not too much to ask, Vanessa."

She hesitated and then smiled at his bride. "Right away, sir."

"Decaf for me, please," Alicia said.

Alicia's dark hair was drawn back from her fine-boned face and held by a pair of fat, gold clips. She wore a dark, tailored suit that made her look elegant but much too thin. Pregnant women were supposed to put on weight, not lose it. Was she all right?

Had she dressed up for him? He wondered because Victor had called him from the Quarter. When Victor had said he'd lost her for a while, he'd described her clothes. She hadn't been wearing a dark suit when she'd gone shopping earlier.

He wouldn't have thought much about her disappearance except he knew that her father had had a mysterious visitor today. A veiled lady. Basil Bienville, the infamous blogger had started the rumor that the woman was Alicia. He'd speculated she'd visited him because today was her birthday.

Vanessa brought in a coffee tray, set it down without asking Alicia if she took cream or sugar and left them.

"Why are you here?" he asked Alicia when they were alone.

Was she here to tell him where she'd gone when she'd disappeared? Wondering if Basil was right, he braced himself for her confession.

"I came because…" She flushed as she poured herself a cup of decaf coffee and watched him with an intensity that made him even more uneasy. She looked guilty of something. Then she said, "Cici called."

"Cici?"

Alicia licked her lips and waited. When he said nothing more, she began in a rush, "She and Logan want us to come to Belle Rose for dinner. She said we should come on a Friday or a Saturday so we could stay the night."

"Do you want to go?"

"They're your family. It's your decision."

"They'd expect us to share a bedroom…and a bed… like a normal, married couple. Is that something you really want to do?"

Her face reddened. "Oh. I didn't think."

She looked away as an answering tide of heat swept him. The dinner invitation was beginning to appeal to him. Yet…

"We plan to separate after the child is born. I think it's unwise to make this more difficult on ourselves or to involve other people, especially my family. We've discussed this before," he said.

"I'll call her and decline."

Damn. "No, leave Cici to me."

Some emotion flashed in her eyes. Then she blushed. "Of course. I understand. You would use any excuse to talk to her, wouldn't you?"

"What's that supposed to mean?"

"Nothing."

When she whitened and turned quickly away, he wondered why she was so upset. Did it bother her that he'd once been in love with Cici? Why be jealous of a relationship that had been dead for years?

"You do still see it that way, that we have to live by the rules we set, don't you?" he said smoothly, hoping she'd indicate she didn't.

"Yes. It's all perfectly logical." Her voice was too soft and her spine too straight, and she was wringing her hands in her lap.

"As if anything in our situation is logical." She was his enemy's daughter, but he wanted her more with every passing day. Wanted her enough to take her home to visit his family—just so he'd have an excuse to share her bed. "Are you sure nothing's wrong?" he asked.

"I'm fine."

"Separate bedrooms was your idea, remember?"

She whirled on him. "I said I'm fine!"

"Then why do you sound upset as hell?"

"I don't know. I don't know anything anymore. It's like my life has spun out of control. My dad getting into trouble. You. The pregnancy. Our marriage. I don't have anything to hold on to."

"Why did Cici's call upset you so much?"

"Who said it did?"

"It did. I can tell."

"I don't know. You've been so nice lately, it's impossible to hate you. And if I can't even hold on to that, what does that leave me?"

"A chance to start over maybe. Look, I heard a rumor that today's your birthday. Is that true?"

She lowered her head shyly and he knew it was.

"Why didn't you tell me?" he whispered.

"We barely know each other. This wasn't supposed to happen."

"What?" he demanded.

She stood up. "I'd better go home so you can work in peace."

He sprang to his feet. "Hey there—you can't just start something and then run. Alicia, I want to know what's going on. Are you jealous of Cici?"

"No!"

She was hell-bent for his door now, so he stopped her the only way he knew how—by clamping a strong hand over her arm and swinging her around into his arms.

"It's you I want. Not her." He tilted her chin, then lowered his gaze to her lips that were so provocatively close to his. He was starving for another kiss. Starving. "Do you ever think about that night? I do. I want to do all the things we did that night again."

When she gazed at his mouth, he said, "I think it's way past time we changed the dynamics of our marriage. Don't normal people in normal relationships just let things progress to the next level sometimes? Like we did *that* night?"

"That's how we got in this mess."

"It's what brought us together. We took risks that night because we wanted each other."

"Everybody who works for you hates me. You don't want me near your family."

"Look, you're my wife, a wife I very much want to get along with better. I'd like us to agree that our being together because of the baby was our start, but maybe that doesn't have to always be the only reason we're together. I know I said we should keep my family out of this if our marriage was going to be temporary. What if I want to change the rules?"

"How? Why?"

"I think it's stupid to plan for failure. Our baby will need us together more after he or she is born. Why don't we give our marriage a chance? What if I call Cici and suggest that since today's your birthday, we'll drive out for dinner Saturday night and have birthday cake with candles and presents, the works…with the whole family? I'll tell her how proud I am of you, that I want to show you off to my family. Then—what if tonight I take you out for dinner, just the two of us, and celebrate your birthday?"

She shook her head. "I—I can't believe you mean this. Not when I'm who I am and you're who you are."

"I don't want to fight. I think it's way past time we started considering new options—other than fighting—don't you?"

He moved to take her into his arms, but before he could touch her, a light knock on the door stopped him cold.

Vanessa swept inside with a stack of documents in her arms. "Oh, I'm so sorry," she exclaimed. "Am I interrupting something?"

Alicia blushed. "No, I was just going."

And just like that, the moment was lost. Jake clenched his hands, then forced himself to unclench them.

"Don't go," he whispered to his wife, who froze.

"Sorry," Vanessa said softly as she set the documents on his desk.

"Me, too," he muttered.

When Vanessa tiptoed outside, Jake turned back to his wife. "I'd very much like a fresh start."

"I would, too. If only such a thing were possible."

"I believe we have to make our own opportunities," he said, his hungry gaze on her beautiful lips again.

Leaning into her, he put his hands on her shoulders and drew her closer. A pulse was beating madly in her throat.

"Happy birthday," he murmured, caressing her arms in an effort to ease her tension.

Her eyes lit up.

Seizing his chance, he kissed her. She expelled a delicious sigh and clasped him tighter.

The kiss went on and on. Finally her dark eyes opened slowly and rose to his. He ran a light fingertip down her cheek. "Nice," he whispered.

Long after she'd said goodbye and left him, her taste and scent lingered.

The hours dragged. He couldn't wait to get home.

Twelve

The SUV was speeding along the Interstate lined on both sides by moss-covered live oaks and cypress trees and the occasional chemical plant. Not that Alicia was paying much attention to the semitropical abundance of greenery. She was too conscious of her husband behind the wheel. Ever since her birthday, he'd made it plain how much he wanted her.

She wanted him, too, but reckless sex was what had caused their problems. If they were going to parent a child, their relationship needed to be based on something deeper than mere animal attraction. He needed to like her and respect her. They needed to trust each other. That said, she'd taken great pains with her hair and makeup and white linen dress.

"Why do you keep fidgeting with the strap of your purse?" he asked.

"I'm not fidgeting." She pushed the straw purse onto

the floorboard, so she wouldn't be tempted to keep tracing the rough edges of the stitched leather strap.

"We don't have to go to Belle Rose, you know. My family always makes me feel…"

"What? How do they make you feel?"

"Let's just say I'd rather spend the weekend alone with you. I'll turn around. We'll call Cici on my cell."

"No. They've probably already cooked dinner for us."

"So, they can eat it themselves and have more leftovers to enjoy."

"You know that people always go to more trouble for guests. They spend hours doing all sorts of things they'd never do otherwise."

"Things they need to do."

"I don't want to be rude to your family just because I feel nervous about going there pretending I'm your wife."

"You *are* my wife. I told you I'd like to try to make this work."

Heat washed over her. When she made no comment, he didn't push as he often did, and for that she should have been grateful. But when he didn't speak to her until he pulled into the oak alley that led up to the pillared mansion where he'd grown up, she grew more nervous.

The deep shade and banks of flowers made the house look like something out of a dream. Could they make a go of it? Would she ever feel she belonged here?

"I'd forgotten how beautiful your boyhood home is."

His knuckles were white; his face was tense. "I never forgot, no matter how long I stayed away. And believe me, I tried. Time and again I told myself I'd never come back here. There was too much emotion to deal with."

"So, here we are," she said lightly.

He parked as far as possible from the house, maybe so his family wouldn't hear the car and come out to greet them. Was he trying to put off seeing them for as long as possible?

Sunlight sifted through the trees and leaves crackled underneath her feet as they walked through the humid heat up to the house, pulling their overnight bags behind them.

"It's not quite so hot here as it is in the city," she said, trying to lighten the mood with conversation again.

He nodded but didn't elaborate.

Like a child eager for Christmas morning, Noonoon must have been watching for Jake. No sooner had he planted one long foot on the bottom stair that led up to the veranda than she opened the door in a rush and hurled herself into Jake's arms.

"Mister Jake, you don't get home near often enough." Her dark eyes shone with pleasure.

After a moment, he said, "Have you met my wife, Alicia?"

"We met before," Noonoon said, smiling as she released Jake so he could include Alicia in a three-way hug.

When his family heard the commotion, they spilled out onto the veranda too. Hayes Daniels, Logan's CEO and best friend, who was tall and dark, was with them. Alicia wasn't too thrilled to see him, because he'd been a key player in bringing her father down. She avoided his stony gaze. Obviously he didn't approve of her. Logan kept his distance—maybe because they'd dated in the past.

Cici had a red scarf in her curls, gold earrings dangling from her ears and gold bangles on her arms. She wore a soft white dress. The skirt swirled around her slim ankles every time she moved, and she moved a lot. She looked beautiful and wild and too thrilled to see Jake. Or was she simply so exuberant because she was newly married herself?

Hard to tell for Alicia, since the green monster held her in thrall.

Everybody talked and laughed at once—nervously, Alicia thought. Was that because they were all trying too hard?

More hugs were exchanged, and it seemed to Alicia that Jake embraced Cici much longer than he held anyone else. When Jake released Cici, did Alicia imagine that Logan and Jake barely shook hands? Jake was definitely ill at ease around his family, especially his brother.

Logan took their bags and carried them upstairs. Even though Alicia had always longed for a close, loving family, her spirits sank every time Cici smiled at Jake.

Then Pierre, who was eighty, hobbled up to Alicia on a cane and told her how glad he was to see her again. He alone seemed relaxed and unaware of any familial undercurrents.

Taking her hand in his cool, shaky grip, he led her inside and invited her to sit beside him so that he could get a good look at her. Jake joined them. Logan returned and put his arm around Cici and held her possessively on the other side of the room. Cici, her eyes alight, tossed her blond curls back and kissed her husband on the cheek. She did seem to be deeply in love with Logan.

Although Jake's family asked her questions about her life as a new bride, Alicia felt so shy and tongue-tied that Jake did most of the talking. He told them how she'd improved his backyard. He spoke of their evenings out at some of the better New Orleans restaurants, making it sound as if they were truly and happily married.

Acting the part, she smiled while he talked. Maybe he really did want to make their marriage work. Gradually she relaxed. With all her heart she longed to be the happy, carefree couple he described even as she wondered if it would ever be possible.

"When are you going to go on a honeymoon?" Hayes Daniels asked suspiciously as Noonoon served the first course.

"What do you think, darling?" Jake brushed Alicia's fingertips with his lips. "After things settle down? Maybe in eight or nine months?"

Dazzled by his expectant gaze and unexpected touch, she couldn't think straight. The baby might be old enough to leave for a long weekend by then she thought—if they were still together. *If* was the key word.

"Who knows?" she whispered.

"You two seem so good together," Logan said. "And to think I never saw it coming."

Guilt made Alicia's pulse quicken.

"It took us by surprise, too," Jake said.

"Funny how things work out," Hayes added as he turned to Jake. "You and Mitchell Butler's daughter together. You were so angry that morning we went to the feds."

"Yes I was."

"Well, it's good having you back in Louisiana, Jake," Logan said. "Now that you're settled, do you think you'll stay awhile? There's still a lot to rebuild."

"A year ago I would have said no unequivocally," Jake said.

"And now?"

"Would it matter? You've always been busy with Claiborne Energy. You never needed me."

"You're wrong. That was just your perception of the way things were," Logan said. "The truth is Grand-père and I regretted our part in the estrangement. We're glad you're back in Louisiana, and all of us want you to stay. On a side note, we've decided we need a bigger building for our headquarters downtown and we want you to design it."

"That's wonderful," Alicia said, smiling until she looked at Jake and saw that he wasn't.

"I'd prefer not to discuss the past or business tonight," he said.

Logan nodded. "So I'll call you Monday."

"Fine."

Cici smiled at Alicia. "We think you're a wonderful addition to the family. Logan, can I please please tell her our news?"

When he nodded, she beamed. "I'm pregnant! That's why I'm wearing this full skirt. We felt the baby move this morning."

Wistfully Alicia placed her hand on her abdomen. She hadn't yet experienced that.

"Congratulations," Jake said even as his gaze followed her hand.

He made a toast. "To the future. To more babies in the family."

Alicia blushed when all eyes focused on her. No sooner was dinner over than Noonoon brought in a white birthday cake with candles. Then everybody, including Noonoon, sang "Happy Birthday" to Alicia.

Their radiantly smiling faces blurred as emotion overwhelmed her.

"Thank you," she whispered. "I've never had such a wonderful birthday celebration."

"Wait, we have a birthday present for you, too." Cici handed Alicia a small white box wrapped with gold ribbon.

The tiny card on the gift read, "With love to our new sister, Alicia." "The earrings inside belonged to Logan's and Jake's great-grandmother."

After Alicia tore the paper off, she held her breath when she saw the exquisite diamond earrings inside the box.

"Françoise, our grandmother, didn't want to be accused of pride or vanity, so she painted them black. That was about one hundred years ago."

Alicia smiled.

"The earrings were Pierre's idea, but Jake was in on it, too," Logan said.

"But they should go to Cici," Alicia said.

"I have her ring," Cici said.

"Even so, I…I can't accept them."

"Why not?" Jake asked.

"Because this isn't…real! Because…"

"What isn't real?" Logan looked confused. "I can assure you, the stones are genuine. We had the last of the black paint removed by a professional, but they're real."

"That's not what I meant!"

Jake was frowning at her as he took her hand and pressed her fingertips.

"Look, this was very kind of all of you. But I—I need a minute. To freshen up. Where's our guest room?"

"Down the hall," Cici said. "Then you go upstairs. First door on the right. Are you sure you're feeling well? Do you want me to take you up to it?"

"No! If you'll just excuse me, I'll find it on my own. I'll be fine in a minute."

Folding her napkin into a perfect square and placing it on the table to the left of her plate very precisely, Alicia stood. As soon as she'd escaped the brilliantly lit dining room and their concerned faces, she took in a deep breath and tried to calm down.

She was beginning to want it all—love, a real marriage, a future. Jake had said he wanted to try to make their relationship work, and now his family was being so accepting. And yet her father and all the crimes he was accused of stood between them. Part of her wanted to do as Jake said he wanted and go with the flow, but another part was afraid to trust in her wildest hopes.

Walking down the hall and up the stairs, she opened the door of their guest room and sat down on the bed. She shut her eyes and was fighting to control her conflicting emotions when the door opened and closed, and she heard heavy footsteps striding toward her.

"What's wrong now?" Jake said from behind her.

She whirled. "I can't lie anymore—at least not to your family. I certainly can't take family heirlooms."

"You're the mother of my child. That's real. I want you to have the earrings."

"No. It will be easier if we break up if I never wear them and treasure them as a gift from you and your family. Don't you see, it will be one less thing to lose?"

He was silent for a long moment. "All right. I can understand that. I'll talk to my family. But while we're on the subject of lying, I have a question." His gaze had hardened. "Did you go visit your father on your birthday?"

Swallowing a quick breath, she shut her eyes briefly and then looked away from him. "Yes."

He hissed in air.

"I'm sorry."

"One of the terms of our marriage was that you would stay away from him."

"I couldn't."

"Damn it, you agreed."

"I know. But he called me. Usually he ignores my birthday. It meant a lot to me that he called—and wanted to see me."

"So why didn't he ignore it this year? What did he really want? He wanted something. I'd bet money on it."

She cringed when she remembered the pin hidden under her mattress. She wanted to tell him about that, but she couldn't—not without hurting her father. Not without making a mess of everything.

"What we feel for each other is too fragile to withstand all the pressures from the outside world," she said. "I'm Mitchell Butler's daughter. You couldn't possibly ever really care…" She hated the passion that had crept into her soft voice, exposing her vulnerability as well as her most heartfelt longings.

"I care," he whispered, his low tone heavier and huskier suddenly. "You don't really want me to go, do you?"

She took a quiet pleasure in him asking her that, even though she knew she should tell him to go.

"I don't intend to leave," he whispered.

He leaned down. When he stroked the length of her spine, his warm, caressing hands caused an involuntary shiver. "We've both fought this too long."

"J-Jake, you have to go." Not that she tried to twist

away. His touch was too pleasant, too consoling. Too sexually arousing. In seconds he had her on fire.

"What I have to do is kiss you," he said.

"We have to go back down!"

She felt his hand stroke up the length of her spine again. Then he turned her around. When his gaze locked with hers, his hand moved to her neckline. Slowly he began to unbutton her white linen dress.

Staring into his eyes again, she couldn't resist the hot, naked desire she saw there.

"Here. Now," he whispered.

Thirteen

His mouth was on her breast. "Delicious birthmark," he murmured.

To his surprise she arched her back to draw him nearer. Not only was she not putting up a struggle, but her pulse was beating faster and faster.

Her hands came up and cupped his rough chin. Slowly her soft fingertips guided his mouth down to hers. He knew longing when he saw it. Her eyes burned with need. Her fingertips shook.

"You're as ravenous as I am," he whispered.

"No…"

"Wanna bet?"

He could feel the tension in her even as her warm lips that quivered under his made him want more. He ran his hands through her soft hair soothingly. He knew he should probably let her go, but he wanted her too much.

He'd been on his own so damn long…and so had

she. In a way they were alike, fearing attachment for different reasons. She'd sought love and had never found it, while he'd hated being manipulated by those who'd loved him and had a habit of running if anybody got close.

Her hands and lips fell away. "I don't want to play sexual games," she said, but her voice was a velvet purr that lured him.

"I'm not playing games." His lips slid down her throat to the other nipple that he'd neglected before. He began to suck it in a leisurely way until it was wet and flushed and hard and she lay trembling beneath him.

"You don't want me for anything but sex," she whispered.

"Lucky you," he teased.

"This isn't a game. If we don't go back down soon… what will your family think?"

"That we're newlyweds. That I can't keep my hands off you, which is all too true."

He wanted to touch her, to kiss her, to feel her silken flesh beneath his, to feel the muscles of her legs contract around his waist when he first entered her. He wanted to make her writhe and explode with passion at the exact same moment he did. He wanted to crush her close, to possess her completely again and again, for the next forty years.

That last thought stunned him. It wasn't that he no longer cared if her last name was Butler or that her father had robbed him and ruined his hard-won reputation. Still, for her, he would throw everything away and start over. He wanted to make this work even though he knew it wouldn't be easy.

He kissed Alicia on the mouth again, taking his time, nibbling her lips until her hands began to roam his body and she began to kiss him back. Her lips parted to accept his tongue. As always she tasted like honey. His mouth didn't leave hers until she was making little moans of ecstasy and begging him for much more than chaste kisses.

"I want you inside me," she whispered, hunger making her voice rasp and her eyelids droop lazily.

When he slid his body over hers and probed her sleek, wet entrance with the tip of his erection, she cried out. He fused his mouth to hers and drove into her. Their tongues mated. Their bodies grew hotter and hotter. With each thrust, her fingers dug into his shoulder and her legs tightened around his waist. Her excitement fed his, pushing him even nearer the edge. When it came, their crisis was mutual and spontaneous, shuddering through them both like a hot wave of pleasure.

With a voice muffled by passion, she said those three little words that shouldn't matter but did. Too profoundly.

"I love you."

He didn't want to hear them, so he tried to blot them out. But she repeated them.

"I love you, Jake. I think I've loved you from the first. I want your child more than I've ever wanted anything. And I want you…like this…close to me…always…again and again. Inside me. I don't want a divorce. I want to be your real wife, and that scares me."

He froze, wishing she'd stop.

Love. Marriage. A lifetime together. Children. Grandchildren.

"Alicia…" He put a fingertip to her lips.

"Okay…okay… I'll stop." But her shining eyes continued to caress him with unguarded emotion for another long moment.

"Sorry I said all that mushy stuff," she whispered as she curled herself into his body.

"Don't worry about it," he said, tracing his thumb around the curve of her earlobe.

She squirmed, and soon he felt hooked by her soft arms and legs that wrapped themselves warmly around his. Slowly the need to answer her in words dissolved as he slipped into a black, welcoming unconsciousness.

When he woke up hours later, she was still there, was breathtakingly lovely as ever in his arms as she slept.

He wanted her again, but if he kissed her, he would awaken her. And she might start asking all those troubling questions he wasn't ready to answer.

He was the one who'd pushed for more, and now that she was trying to take their relationship to the next level, he wasn't sure how to deal with it. Suddenly his marriage to Alicia felt like way more than he'd bargained for.

"What are you doing?" Alicia was standing just inside the bedroom door of Jake's New Orleans home.

Ridiculous question. It was plain as day that he was unpacking his suitcase from their overnight trip and repacking a backpack.

If only she could be as cool and suave as he was. If she were a clever bride maybe she'd be able to ignore his coldness and reserve—hold her tongue and bide her time.

Why did she wear her heart on her sleeve and feel compelled to throw herself at people when she craved their love? Last night he'd made wild, impassioned love to her, and she'd been so profoundly touched she'd told him how she felt.

The first hint that something was wrong had been when she'd awakened at Belle Rose and reached for him and found she was alone in their bed. She'd dressed and run downstairs, only to discover him finishing breakfast with Cici and Logan. As soon as she'd entered the dining room, he'd announced they would leave as soon as she ate breakfast.

"I asked what you are doing," Alicia repeated from his New Orleans doorway as he grabbed a tackle box.

Without so much as a glance her way, he slung a pair of jeans and a frayed plaid shirt into his backpack. "I would think it's pretty obvious. I'm packing."

Gus lay in the middle of his bed, watching them both as he thumped his tail and purred. Alicia resented his simple happiness.

"Why? Are you moving out?"

"No." He didn't look up. "I'll be gone a week at most."

"Going where for a week? I don't understand."

"I need solitude. Why did you go see your father when he called? Because you're made that way. Because you had to. I need to get away."

"Can't we just talk about last night?"

"We can talk when I get back. Maybe then I'll have something to say."

"You're making me crazy."

"I'm sorry. That's not my intention."

"What about your work?"

"Things are slow."

He didn't have to explain that. She knew he and his staff believed she or her father were to blame for most of his firm's business problems. "Okay," she said. "Go. Just tell me where you're going."

"To my cabin in Alaska probably." His voice was harsh and loud.

Alaska? As far as possible, in other words.

She hated herself, because if she'd thought it would do any good she would have gotten on her knees and begged him to stay. She wanted to know what he was thinking and feeling. If she'd thought it would do any good, she would have yelled at him until he told her.

For her, the sex last night had been more than wonderful. She'd felt as if her soul had been welded to his, as if it still was—but he was shutting her out, going to Alaska of all places.

"Okay," she said. "Alaska. I'll let you concentrate on your packing."

As she walked slowly out of his room and then downstairs, her heart constricted.

Alaska. She couldn't believe this. Not after last night.

Sucking in a breath, she decided to brew herself a cup of tea. Fifteen minutes later Alicia was sitting quietly in her rocker on the back porch, sipping from her mug, when she heard him in the kitchen.

He'd married her only because of the baby. He'd wanted sex, but obviously he hadn't wanted her saying she loved him. Well, she had a right to her feelings and a right to express them. And she wasn't going to take any of it back. She would just have to deal with this, and so would he.

Not that it was fun. No—she was utterly miserable at the thought of him leaving.

She heard the screen door open. Then his footsteps sounded as he approached her. She notched her chin up and met his gaze.

"I don't want to quarrel," he said. "I'm going—so I can figure myself out. Vanessa will call later to check on you."

"I'll be okay."

A muscle pulled in his jaw as he nodded. "Good."

Her stomach tightened. Her mouth felt too dry to speak, but someone she managed to whisper, "Goodbye."

"Goodbye." Slinging his backpack over his shoulder, he walked across the backyard to the garage.

When the garage door went up and his SUV backed out, she stood and walked to the edge of the porch with her hand on her heart.

He stopped, rolled his window down and waved to her.

She took a deep breath and waved back. Then she held up her hand a blew him a kiss.

He nodded mutely. Then his tinted window went up.

When the gate closed behind him and she finally went back inside, the stillness within the house seemed deafening.

Fourteen

Alicia couldn't bear Jake's big, quiet house after he'd left, so she called Carol.

"Why don't you come to London?" Carol said as soon as Alicia had told her everything.

Why couldn't she go somewhere? Who said she was stuck here just because he'd left?

"You're right. I could take a little trip of my own."

Suddenly there was a loud knock at her front door.

"Somebody's outside," Alicia said.

"Maybe it's him—come to his senses."

"He has a key. No, it's either Vanesa or our land-lady."

Curious, Alicia told Carol she'd call her back after she saw who it was, then she hung up.

When she crept to the front of the house and lifted the shade, Vanessa waved at her.

Disappointment swamped Alicia as she cracked the

door. "Okay, you did your job," she said. "I'm fine, so you can go home to your sons."

"They're not there right now. So—are you going to invite me in to your pity party or not?"

"Am I that obvious?"

"Who wouldn't be in your shoes? You're a beautiful bride, and your big dope of a husband runs off to Alaska."

Alicia didn't know what to say, so she stood aside and let Vanessa sweep boldly across her threshold.

"I know Jake asked you to check on me, but it's not necessary. I'm fine."

"I tried to call, but your line was busy. I thought if you were free, maybe we could go out to dinner."

"Like I said, it's not necessary."

"If I'm going to remain Jake's secretary, allow me to disagree. Besides, I'd get brownie points from Jake if you'd say yes."

"He doesn't really care about me."

"Then why did he run all the way to Alaska?"

"He runs as far as he can—and this is proof he cares?"

"I'd put money on it. What did you do to scare the socks off him?"

"Scare him?"

"Don't look so wide-eyed and innocent. I know scared when I see scared. If I didn't know better, I'd say he's in love. He just doesn't know it yet."

Was that true? The image of Jake's large body on top of hers flashed in her mind. He'd felt so wonderful. So right. Everything had been perfect until she'd told him she loved him. Not that she could tell his nosy secretary about their great sex.

"Look…er…" Alicia began.

"Okay, I get it. What if I promise to quit prying into my boss's love life, not to mention yours? Will you say yes to dinner then?"

Vanessa probably knew Jake better than anybody else. If she thought he was scared, maybe Alicia could learn more about what scared him if she spent time with this woman. Besides, she was friendly and seemed like fun.

"It's not like I have anything better to do," Alicia said.

"What do you say we exact revenge on your honey and go somewhere really, really expensive? I mean somewhere I could never afford on what he pays me?"

Alicia laughed. "I'll get dressed." A wild idea had begun to germinate in the back of her mind.

"Do you know where exactly he is in Alaska?" Alicia asked.

"Who do you think made arrangements for his favorite bush pilot to drop him and a week's worth of supplies up at his cabin south of Denali National Park? He goes there every year around this time in the summer. He says the place clears his mind."

"What does he do there?"

"It's wild country. He hunts and fishes. Not my thing, but he always returns tanned and happier. Some summers I can actually stand him for a whole month. The year he broke a bone in his knee when he fell running from a grizzly he was happy for three months. You know what I heard him say? 'I had fun. I nearly died.' *Men!*"

"What if I wanted to join him for a…er…a belated honeymoon? Could you make the same arrangements for me?"

The idea that had begun to germinate as Alicia was

getting dressed blossomed. Suddenly she knew exactly where she wanted to spend the next week and what she wanted to do.

"His cabin doesn't have electricity or running water. You have to carry water from the river to bathe. And like I said, it's grizzly bear country."

"I really want to understand him, I need to make this trip."

"You know what they say—if you love him let him go. If he doesn't come back, hunt him down and kill him."

"Next time. I'd prefer to surprise him."

"You're one gutsy girl."

"So will you help me?" Alicia asked.

"Can I finish my margarita first? When we're done here, we'll go back to the office, where I have all the phone numbers. Oh…and before we leave, don't let me forget to snap a picture of you and the delectable Javier."

"Who's Javier?"

"Honey, he's the yummy bartender who's been giving me the eye all night."

"Jake said you don't like men."

"Wrong. I've got three children, haven't I?"

Jake was looking forward to a meal of mild-flavored grayling as he laid his heavy stringer of fish on the rocky ground and stared at the cloud-shrouded peaks of the wild range extending east and west as far as he could see. He'd build a fire, sit out in the open and enjoy the view. He was tired after having spent fourteen hours hip-deep in icy rapids fishing.

Sucking in a long breath, he wished Alicia was standing here beside him. He wanted to share with her the extraordinary sensation of freedom and release this big land gave him. Then he frowned as he realized he was thinking of her again.

What was wrong with him? He'd come here to get some distance from his feelings for her, to enjoy the land that had always been such a comfort. So, why couldn't he shake her hold even here? He liked being on his own.

Usually there was nothing like a couple of days in the wild to change his view of the world and make him realize that what had been bothering him back home wasn't really much of a problem.

Twice already he'd let his thoughts of her distract him to the point of endangering himself. He'd gotten too close to a blond grizzly with black legs and a moose intent on gobbling river vegetation right where he wanted to fish. Even though he'd had a gun, he'd let the moose and grizzly have his fishing hole.

Suddenly he heard the thin drone of a single-engine plane flying low, which was odd because few people came up here. His heart leapt. Hill wasn't due back to pick him up for four days, but if he was here dropping another hunter, and if he could wave him down, there was no reason he couldn't return early to his bride.

Scanning the sky, he tried to locate the plane. But no matter how hard he squinted and strained, he never saw the plane. The noise grew fainter and Jake cursed in frustration. When all was silent again, he dropped to his knees. The wilderness felt alien and lonely. He'd had enough of it, and he knew it was because he needed Alicia too much.

She'd said she loved him. His feelings for her were so powerful he was afraid to analyze them. So, he wouldn't.

He'd just live with them and try to get used to them before he put a name on them.

Slowly he picked up his stringer and resumed trudging the last three miles to his cabin that stood on top of the ridge. He was a mile out when he saw wisps of dark smoke curling into the air. Somebody was at his cabin. That somebody had built a fire.

Hugging herself, Alicia stood on the porch of Jake's one-room log cabin. She'd been so sure coming here was the right thing to do.

So sure—until she'd gotten here and Hill had flown away and left her with only the whispery stillness of the trees for company. Without Jake she felt too alone.

Was it only an hour ago that she'd fibbed bravely to Hill that Jake was expecting her, and, no, Hill didn't have to wait and make sure she was all right, that he could take off?

"He didn't say nothin' about you coming," Hill had insisted, repeating that he'd be glad to wait. "He always comes by hisself."

Her heart had quickened but she'd said, "Our plans were tentative, like I told you."

He'd cocked a bushy eyebrow and had eyed her suspiciously. "I'll even stay the night if you like. I can sleep in my plane. You wouldn't even know I was here. Unless there was trouble."

"He'll be here."

"All right, then. If you're sure… Tell you what—I'll do a flyby tomorrow just to make sure you're all right." He'd instructed her as to what hand signals to use to wave him down or send him on his way. "Don't want to land unnecessarily," he'd said gruffly. "Waste of fuel."

Without further ado he'd taken off for Fairbanks.

She'd toted the single bag Hill had allowed her to fly with to the cabin and had busied herself gathering wood and building a fire, all the while keeping an eye out for any kind of bear. Not just a grizzly.

"There's no such thing as a good bear in Alaska," Hill had warned her. "They're all wild and unpredictable, especially this time of year. And don't leave any food out."

She felt sick to her stomach with worry. What if Jake was furious? What if he hated her for following him?

So what? He was her husband. She had to know what he felt. That's why she'd come here. She had to know if they had a chance. Every day she was investing more of herself into this marriage.

Suddenly she glimpsed movement against the horizon—a tiny figure was heading purposefully for the cabin. Maybe a lone moose or caribou, she told herself, trying not to get her hopes up that it was Jake, even as she hoped that it was.

Finally she made out a tall man with long legs and a familiar gait. *Jake.* He had something heavy slung over a broad shoulder that caused him to lean to one side as he strode toward her.

"Jake? Jake!" She tore down the steps and ran toward him. *"Jake!"*

He must have heard her. After a pause, he started running, too. She was breathless when they both stopped a few yards from each other.

Without taking his eyes off her, he knelt and carefully laid his fat stringer of heavy fish on the ground.

"Nice fish," she whispered, feeling uncertain suddenly.

He stood again and contemplated the fish and then the scuffed toes of his boots for a long moment.

"I got lucky. Real lucky." His gaze climbed her slowly, lingering on her mouth, and she didn't think he was talking about his catch.

She hissed in a breath. Was he really as glad to see her as she was to see him? His handsome face was flushed. His chocolate-brown hair fell across his brow. She swallowed, waited.

A sheepish grin crept across his features as he reached for her. The fierce emotion that tore through him, causing him to shudder as he pulled her to him, shredded her, too.

Giving a little cry, she smothered her lips in his thick hair, which smelled of wood smoke and damp forest.

"So what are you doing way up here?" he whispered huskily in an odd voice he'd never used before. When she didn't answer at first, his grip around her body tightened.

She was thrilled that he kept holding her, but still afraid that once he got over the shock that she was here, he might be angry.

"Are you all right?" he demanded. "Is the baby all right?"

"Yes! I had to come. I had to know what you felt. I couldn't go on loving you, wondering if you hate me, or if I'm too clingy and not what you want. I know I shouldn't have chased you, and I'll stay out of your way while I'm here."

"Shut up." His voice was suddenly so harsh and cold, she was terrified that as soon as he was sure the baby was okay, he was going to send her away. She felt his arms knot with tension. For a long moment he said nothing else.

"What am I going to do about you?" His arms

tightened around her shoulders and he pulled her closer.

"I know I probably shouldn't have come," she whispered. "I should have never have suggested marriage…and made you feel so trapped that you had to run all the way up here."

"What?" Suddenly he burst out laughing.

"Don't laugh at me," she begged. "Whatever you do, don't laugh."

"I'm not laughing at you. I'm glad you're here, you little fool. I missed you hellishly. I admire your honesty. I was an ass. It took a lot of guts on your part to come here. But I'm glad you did."

"You are?"

"*Very* glad. I kept saying I wanted to take our relationship to the next level. I guess I got my wish. And for the record, I'm not talking just about sex."

As Alicia clung to him, her eyes filled with tears of joy.

"Don't cry," he whispered.

"It's just that I'm so happy."

Leaning down, he cupped her chin. Gently he brushed her trembling lips with his own, and a wild piercing joy such as she had never known filled her. When he deepened the kiss, Alicia's knees went limp.

A long time later he said, "Let's go inside. Unless you want me looking over your shoulder for a grizzly the whole time we're making love."

She laughed and he let go of the long dark strands of her hair that had become tangled in his fist at her nape.

"I was wishing that I'd brought you with me," he said. "I wanted to share all this with you so much."

I love you, she thought, but this time she knew better than to say it aloud.

He didn't say it either, and he probably wasn't close to thinking it, but the light in his eyes every time he looked at her coupled with the thrilled grin that dazzled her was enough.

At least for now.

Fifteen

Jake brought the fish inside and set them in his ice cooler.

"I'll clean them later." He turned to her. "You can't leave anything edible outside here—including your delectable self."

"Hill told me that."

"That old rascal...flying you here and leaving you all alone.... What if I'd been camping out?"

"He didn't want to. And he promised to fly over and check on me tomorrow."

"Well, you're not giving the orders from now on. You're not to go outside—not without me—ever. Especially not at night, even though it only gets dark for an hour...and not completely dark even then."

"Bears?"

"This is wild country."

Alicia's confidence soared. He was obviously glad

she was here and he was being so protective. Maybe he didn't love her, but he definitely felt something.

"Come here," he whispered.

She hesitated but only for a moment. "Aren't you starving? You've been fishing all day. And you walked…"

"We'll eat later. After…"

"After what?" she teased.

"I'm hungrier for you than for anything else. The past two days felt like the longest in my life. You're becoming a habit."

"Is that all I am?"

"Withdrawal was hell." His laugh was husky and tinged with desire. "Worst of all, I think you're beginning to know your power over me."

"Is it so hard to trust me?" Would her father always be between them?

Jake didn't answer.

When he took her in his arms, she closed her eyes at the surge of joy that filled her. With calloused fingers rasping across her silken skin he slowly removed her clothes. First he unbuttoned her blouse and then reached inside her waistband and unsnapped her jeans and pulled both jeans and satin panties down. Last he unhooked her lacy black bra so that her breasts swung free. Then it was her turn to strip him. She couldn't tear off his clothes fast enough, tossing them in heap on top of hers.

She swept her hand over his flat stomach and pectoral muscles. Sinking to her knees she began to use her mouth.

He sucked in a savage breath when the tip of her tongue stroked the length of his erection. "Not yet," he whispered raggedly, dragging her down onto a low cot draped with his sleeping bag.

"Still scared of losing control?" she teased.

"Who me? No, I just want to take my time…and make you happy, too."

"I am happy."

"Happier then."

But in the end, he couldn't wait any more than she could. When he plunged inside her, she wrapped her legs around him and held on tight. As he began to move in that rhythmical dance as ancient as time, she grew hotter and wetter until finally she couldn't bear it and they exploded together, waves of passion crashing over them.

The second time he let her please him with her mouth. The third time he took her hard and fast again. After the fourth, they were so tired they slept curled against each others' bodies. When they woke up, it was still light.

"I'm starving," he said. "Time to clean the fish and build a fire. Time to feed you."

"I brought a jar of peanut butter and jelly and two loaves of bread," she whispered. "Just in case…"

"Cheater."

"Appetizers," she amended.

He laughed. "Smart girl. Let's make sandwiches. Who wants to clean fish when I can lie in bed holding you?"

He wasn't professing love, but he wasn't indifferent. That was something, wasn't it?

"Alicia! Wake up! You've got to see this!"

At first she was so groggy, she was afraid something was wrong, but when he crashed back into the cabin without bothering to shut the door, her worry dissolved.

Wrapping her in a blanket, he led her by the hand

across the rough planks of the floor to the porch. Once there, he put his arm around her and hugged her close.

"It's the northern lights," he said. "You almost never see them in the summer. The sky isn't dark enough for long enough."

Undulating ribbons of light shimmered against the horizon. Streaks of green, orange, yellow and dark red danced like flame.

Together, in silence, they enjoyed the miraculous display that seemed like it had been designed for them alone.

"I feel like we're the last man and woman on earth," she finally said.

"Adam and Eve in the Garden of Paradise?"

"Sort of. But since they were naked, I always imagined their paradise as being tropical."

"We got naked."

"In a cabin."

When the display ended, he took her back to bed and made love to her again.

Then it was over and he held her close, caressing her hair and silken skin.

"I wish we never had to go home," she said.

"Me, too. But we do, of course," he murmured.

"Like Adam and Eve thrown out of paradise?"

"So I did make you happy."

"Very happy. So happy."

And yet some part of her still felt unsure when she thought about their future.

It was midnight. Except for a sliver of brilliant silver light fringing the horizon, low, dark clouds wrapped Fairbanks International Airport. Since their jet to the lower forty-eight was late, Alicia had had time to charge her cell phone, its battery having run down up at the cabin. No service.

When she checked it after charging it and saw that her father had called repeatedly, leaving several increasingly urgent messages begging her to call him, alarm made her heart pound.

"Jake, I'll just be a minute," she said, pointing toward the ladies' room.

He nodded absently and went back to his newspaper.

When her father didn't answer any of the numbers he'd left and his home phone indicated that his home number had been disconnected, she tried to ignore the sinking feeling in the pit of her stomach. Had the stress gotten to him? Had he had a heart attack or something? Even though it was the middle of the night in Louisiana, wouldn't he have answered his phone if he was okay?

Reluctantly she slipped her phone into a pocket of her purse and returned to Jake.

"What's wrong?" He looked up from his paper and studied her much too closely.

Twisting a strand of her hair, she glanced away uneasily. For the first time in days, she thought about the pin her father had slipped into her shopping bag and that she'd hidden. She hadn't tried to return it because she hadn't wanted to get him into more trouble. Or complicate her situation with Jake. Now she wished she'd marched back to her father's house, sans scarves, and had handed it over to the guard the same day she'd discovered it.

If her father was okay, she'd do that as soon as they got back to New Orleans. From now on she wanted to be honest with Jake about everything. He was her future.

"What's this little worry line between your brows?" Jake asked, gently touching it. "Why won't you look at me?"

When she pulled back, his hand fell to his newspaper.

She bit her lips. "It's about my father. He tried to call me—repeatedly. I just tried to call him back, but he doesn't answer. I know it's the middle of the night in Louisiana, but he should be home. I'm afraid something's happened to him."

Jake's gaze was hard and piercing as he pulled his own cell phone out of his pocket and snapped it open. "I'll call Logan. Maybe he knows something."

"Okay," she whispered tightly.

Their time in Alaska had been the next best thing to a honeymoon. They'd spent days hiking and fishing and exploring. He'd shown her all his favorite fishing holes and vistas. At night they'd cooked outside and then had made love in the cabin before a glowing fire until all hours. She'd given herself to him completely, hoping that he'd break down and do the same. He'd come close a time or two, but somehow he'd always held some part of himself in check.

Even so, she hadn't wanted their special time to end, but now it had—with a bang.

As she watched him punch in Logan's number, her throat felt dry. Suddenly there was a bad taste in her mouth.

Shortly into his call to her brother, he shot her a dark look that told her the news wasn't good. Jake's face grew increasingly tense as he listened. His own replies were so cryptic and terse, she couldn't tell what was going on. Something was definitely up. Then he said goodbye and shoved his phone into his breast pocket.

She inhaled a long breath. "What's going on?"

"Your father has violated the terms of his parole and fled to Brazil. Apparently he'd distributed lots of valuables to people he was close to."

"Valuables?" she repeated in a croaky voice. Her first guilty thought concerned her mother's pin.

"Jewelry. Diamonds. Cash. He went to certain people before he left and asked that his property be returned. When they complied, he left the country. For good. Of course, the feds consider the money and diamonds theirs."

"Oh, no! Not before his trial! This makes him look… so guilty."

"Yes. It does. You've got to face the fact that he ran because he's guilty. He intends to sell the diamonds and live in Brazil. The last thing he's ever wanted is justice! Or you!"

She shut her eyes, but she could not shut out the horrible truth. If her father wasn't guilty, who else could have done what he'd been accused of? Why had he run?

"Did he give you money? Or diamonds? Did he? Because if he did, you'd better call the feds and tell them right now."

Watching him, she chewed her lips, feeling torn and uncertain about Logan's news. Slowly the last illusion about her father that she'd clung to dissolved. He had to be guilty.

"Jake, I just need to sit here quietly and digest this."

"Fine. You do that."

He turned his back and pretended to read his paper. She knew he was pretending, because he never turned a page. He just sat there, statue still, his spine rigid, fighting to ignore her.

She'd been fooling herself. They'd never had a chance. There was too much between them. She was Mitchell Butler's daughter, and therefore doomed forever to be his enemy.

As soon as they got home, she would call that awful agent who'd evicted her from her apartment and tell him she had her mother's pin.

Jake would never believe that she hadn't taken it on purpose.

He would never forgive her.

She would face that when they were home in New Orleans.

Sixteen

Alicia was anxiously unpacking in her downstairs bedroom when the doorbell chimed. She rushed out into the hall, but Jake was already stomping down the stairs ahead of her, taking them two and three at a time, with Gus trotting behind him.

"I'll get it," she said.

"No, I will," he replied, not looking at her.

"But it's for me," she whispered.

They'd barely spoken on the long flight home or on the shorter taxi ride to the house. She was dead with exhaustion, sick with worry about her father and her relationship with Jake. On top of all that, she dreaded this interview that she'd set up with the federal agent from Seattle when they'd landed to change planes.

Gus's silken tail curved around her legs as she stood in the hall and waited as Jake opened the door.

"FBI," said a familiar voice. "Is Mrs. Claiborne home?"

"What do you want with her?"

"I'm here to question her about her father, Mitchell Butler."

"She's been in Alaska on a honeymoon with me, so she's not involved with his flight to Brazil."

"She did call us and set this appointment up herself."

"What?"

"From Seattle," she whispered, walking slowly to Jake's side. "As soon as I heard the facts about my father, I knew there was something I had to tell this man. And you."

Jake stood where he was, statue still, his face blank and cold.

Her heart sank. He would never believe that she hadn't taken the pin deliberately because she'd intended to help her father escape.

"I'd prefer that she have an attorney present," Jake said, surprising her.

The self-righteous FBI agent who'd evicted her lifted his bulbous nose and stared at her so accusingly through his wire-rimmed glasses, she began to feel a little faint.

She must have whitened, because Jake slid a protective arm around her. Then he suggested everybody sit down in the living room. Flat-eared, Gus hunched down on all fours and watched the agent with wary yellow eyes.

The agent leaned toward her. "Why don't we get to the point? Why exactly did you call us?"

She felt Jake tense beside her.

"On the morning of my birthday my father called me and said he wanted to wish me a happy birthday.

He invited me over, so I went. While I was there, he tried to give me a birthday gift, a pin I've always loved that belonged to my mother. I refused to take it, but somehow, I don't know how, he managed to hide it in one of my shopping bags. I didn't discover it until I got home."

Jake's hand on her shoulders fell away. She was aware of him stiffening rigidly beside her.

"As you may remember," the agent said, his eyes on both of them, "when your father agreed to the terms of his house arrest, he signed papers saying he would give no assets of any kind away. Not to you. Not to anybody."

"I really think she needs an attorney present," Jake said.

"Our sources think he gave you diamonds," the agent persisted.

"He gave me an heirloom pin that had belonged to my mother. I've been trying to figure out how to return it to him without making things worse for him."

Jake sucked in a breath and stood up. Then he strode to a far corner of the room, where he stared coldly out the window.

"Your father was in no position to give you anything—as I've explained to you repeatedly, in some detail. Isn't that right?" the agent demanded.

"Yes," she whispered.

"So you knew you should have called us immediately," he said. "Didn't you?"

"Yes."

"May I see it—the gift?"

Slowly she got up and went to her room. Within minutes she returned with the lacquered box. The agent took it and opened it. He removed the pin and then tossed it to her impatiently as he continued to manhandle the box.

Turning it over, he shook it.

"There's nothing in it," she said just as he opened a secret drawer and removed a small envelope.

"Nothing, you say?" He began unfolding the tissue paper. As he pulled back the last bit of paper, hundreds of diamonds caught the light and shot sparks.

"Nothing?" The agent whistled. "Investment grade, if I'm not mistaken," he said, lifting his hard gaze to hers.

Slowly he rewrapped the tissue around the diamonds and returned them to the envelope. He replaced the envelope in the box. Last of all, he took her mother's pin from her and put it in the top drawer.

She turned to Jake, but his back was to her as he stood frozen at the window.

"I knew I shouldn't have kept the pin, Jake, and like I said, I didn't intend to keep it. But I didn't know those diamonds were there. I didn't!"

"I'm sure your father would say the same thing." The agent snapped the lid of the box shut.

"Don't say another word to this man, Alicia. Not without my attorney present," Jake said.

"Good day, Mrs. Claiborne. We'll be contacting you very soon." He nodded in Jake's direction. "Mr. Claiborne, I will give you the benefit of the doubt and assume you knew nothing about this."

Jake's icy gaze swept over her.

"Of course, he didn't," Alicia said. "He wanted me to have nothing to do with him."

"You should have listened to your husband."

* * *

Her heart full of pain, Alicia stared into those cold blue eyes she no longer recognized.

"Jake, I swear I didn't know the diamonds were there," she said.

"Save your breath," he said in a low, hard tone.

"All my life I wanted my father to love me. I wanted to believe maybe he'd softened…that maybe the birthday gift really meant something. Just like I thought Alaska meant something."

"You're unbelievable! You know what? You almost had me believing that Alaska meant something, too. Now I don't know. Funny, when people lie to you, it's hard to know where the lies end and the truth begins. All I know is that I want out of this marriage."

"My father knew how much I loved my mother and how much I would treasure that pin," she said brokenly. "I really was planning to take it back."

"Your father wanted to use you to hide portable wealth, and you went along with him. You let him use you."

"You're right. I did. I should have returned that pin that day." Her stomach knotted in pain. She bit her lips. "Maybe…deep down…I knew his having hidden that pin showed how dishonest he was, but he was my father. I've spent my whole life trying to believe in him."

"I'll do what I can, hire you the best lawyers to help you get out of this mess he's caused. But I'm moving out."

"When?"

"Now." Without looking at her again he turned and headed for the stairs.

A rising tide of pain enveloped her. He was leaving

her. Forever. She didn't want Jake to go, but how could she stop him?

When he came back down the stairs, he was carrying a suitcase.

"Until our marriage ends officially, we live apart," he said. "I should have listened to you. You were right about us not having a real marriage."

He turned his back on her then and headed toward the kitchen. Silently she watched his broad shoulders disappear down the hall. Their marriage was over, and it was her fault.

A door opened and closed. Then she was alone.

For a moment as she thought of a lifetime without him, her throat was so tight she felt like she might strangle.

"I can't think about that now," she thought, hugging herself. "I have to think about our baby. I have to be strong for our baby."

Suddenly there was tiny movement like the wings of a butterfly in her abdomen.

The baby. She'd felt their baby.

When their precious child kicked her again, she smiled.

"You don't look too good, boss man," Vanessa said as she dumped a stack of file folders onto his desk.

"What's this?" he growled as he picked up a folder.

"Maybe you should call your wife. She doesn't look so hot either."

Jake had given Vanessa a bonus to check on Alicia every day and report back to him. Because of this she seemed to think he'd given her a license to interfere. "You said she was fine."

"She misses you."

"And you know this how?"

"I know. She's heartbroken, and I'm tired of going over there and seeing her pale face and shadowed eyes. The girl looks haggard, and she resents me…for not being you."

"She crossed a line. She'd not the woman I'd begun to think she was."

"Okay, so what if her father hid a few diamonds in a gift he snuck into her shopping bag. So she didn't tell you, since, big surprise, you've been such a jerk on the subject of her father. I wouldn't have told you either."

"If she's telling the truth, she should have called the feds about that pin as soon as she discovered it. Lots of people probably think I knew she had the diamonds all along. I have no reputation now."

"What about her? She didn't know what that slimeball was up to either, because she's not a criminal. Then after the bastard betrayed her, you walked out on her, too."

"Damn it! That's not how it was! And I'm paying for her legal defense! Why can't you ever, just once, be on my side?"

"I am on your side. That's why I'm telling you to work things out."

"I've got a better idea. Get your nose out of my personal life, so we can get back to work."

She shrugged.

It irritated the hell out of him that Vanessa had been giving him a hard time the past four days. He'd had four miserable nights on Bos's houseboat because he couldn't trust himself to stay in the same city with Alicia and not call her. Alicia had betrayed him. Besides that, she'd reduced him to a needy, clingy, besotted idiot.

Some part of him didn't care if she'd lied to him and

betrayed him. The nights on the houseboat had been even worse than being in Alaska on his own.

The woman had gotten under his skin. She'd hooked him, and no matter how hard he tried to wriggle free, the hook just kept sinking deeper. He'd said he was leaving her. What a joke. He couldn't get through an hour without pining for her.

This was what he'd always feared—that love would take him over again and destroy him as it had before. Only this felt a thousand times worse. He'd fought to become strong and self-reliant. She was a liar and a cheat. Why couldn't he stop wanting her?

Well, he'd said he was finished, hadn't he? He wouldn't go back to her. He wouldn't.

One minute Jake was alone in a jungle of dwarf palmettos and water tupelo as the bull alligators roared and the next he saw a willowy figure paddling a kayak gracefully through the dark waters toward the houseboat.

"Alicia?"

"No, it's just me," Cici said, tossing her blond curls. "Who's the only person crazy enough to follow you into the swamp?"

"Does Logan know where you are?"

"I like to keep him guessing. What are wives for?"

"As long as you don't get me shot."

"He's your brother."

"Right. Family loyalties run deep in the South, and all that rot."

"Deeper than we sometimes realize. You came back, didn't you? And so did I."

She threw him the bowline and he pulled her

kayak snug against the houseboat. Then he helped her disembark. "Want a drink?"

She shook her head. "I just want to talk." She paused. "You've been doing a lot of hiding out…ever since you got married," she said.

"I'd rather not talk about her."

"I'm sure." She hesitated. "Vanessa called me, so I went to see Alicia."

"Vanessa is a real rabble-rouser."

"Alicia's every bit as unhappy as you are."

"The hell I'm unhappy!"

"Right. Just look at you. When was the last time your jaw saw a razor? The only way to end your mutual misery is for you to go back to her."

"She lied."

"You lied, too…about how you feel. Did you ever make her feel like you wanted to marry her? Didn't she have to practically beg you? She had a rotten childhood. Maybe she's tired of begging people to love her."

"That's her problem."

"Then why do you look so awful?"

"Thanks. You look great, by the way."

"Alicia loves you and you love her. You're hurting her terribly because you're so determined to be strong and hard and never care about anybody because you don't want them close enough to hurt you…the way I hurt you. I'm sorry, by the way…."

He didn't say anything.

"But you and me—we're ancient history. What about Alicia, not to mention the baby?" Cici said. "Don't you care that you're hurting them? She told me it moved."

And he hadn't been there.

"What if you're throwing away your one chance at true happiness? Jake, I know what you went through in the past. Believe it or not, I got hurt, too. I ran away and stayed away because I couldn't deal with it. But at some point I learned that maybe there comes a time when you've got to stop running or you'll always have an empty, meaningless life. Sometimes you've got to face who you are and what you need. You're going to be a father. It's obvious to everyone who knows you that you need her. Why don't you forget your pride and put aside your fear of being hurt again? For once in your life—just go for it!"

Seventeen

"Alicia!"

Jake's footsteps rang on the hard floors as he strode through the downstairs shouting her name. His house had never sounded so scarily empty. Usually Gus came trotting up to him when he came home. Not this time.

Where was his wife? And her damned nuisance of a cat? What if she'd already gone to London and taken Gus with her?

Jake tore out the back door and then stopped, expelling a long sigh of relief when he saw a tall, slim woman in a red shirt and jeans tucking a tiny plant into the soft earth as gently as a mother would put a baby to sleep. Alicia's dark, tousled hair fell about her shoulders like a silken veil. She was so damned beautiful. Beside her sat a black-and-white cat, his tail twitching in a lively manner as he eyed a yellow butterfly.

Jake let the screen slam behind him so she'd look

up. She turned as he walked toward her slowly, her eyes widening when she saw him. Their glances touched, held. Neither seemed able to look away.

Finally he stopped at the edge of the lush grass. She stood, warm heat suffusing her cheeks, coloring them prettily. Her eyes were so brilliant and her smile so sweet, he felt a thrilling rush of emotion.

Did she still love him? If so, he would welcome her love and cherish her because he needed her, craved her. She made him feel alive, happy—happy in a way he'd never been happy before.

Clasping her hands together, she waited as he walked across the thick lawn toward her. In the next moment he enfolded her in a crushing embrace.

"Alicia, I've missed you so much!"

She sighed. "I was hoping against hope you'd come back," she whispered breathlessly.

"I'm sorry I walked out on you."

"Your behavior was perfectly understandable under the circumstances."

"That's garbage, and you know it. Forgive me?"

"The minute I saw you standing there." She hesitated. "I love you."

"I can't live without you," he said. "I love you more than anything in the world."

"I think I've been waiting my whole life to feel like this."

He clasped her tightly, burying his face against the smooth skin of her warm, silky throat, inhaling her sweet scent.

She took his hand and placed it on her tummy so that he could feel their baby kick.

"Wow," he whispered.

She was his wife, his love, his everything. He couldn't wait to take her to bed.

He handed her a black velvet box. "I have something for you."

She opened it and expelled an amazed breath. "My mother's pin! How did you get this?" With reverent fingers she caressed each point of the sparkling star just as she used to when she'd been a little girl.

"Let's just say that it cost me a fortune to buy it before the feds' auction, but you're worth it. The feds are going to let you off the hook, too. It took a few legal maneuvers, but we cut a deal."

"Oh, Jake," she whispered clutching the diamond pin to her heart.

He handed her a second velvet jewelry box.

"What's this?"

"My grandmother's earrings. You wouldn't take them when my family gave them to you for your birthday."

She laughed. "I couldn't accept them when I thought our marriage wasn't real."

Holding the box, she hurled herself into his arms and held on tight.

He folded her against his chest, crushing her against him. "I want to design you a house with lots of bedrooms…so we'll have room for more children."

Unable to speak, she stared up at him, her eyes shining with such excitement that he knew she had to feel the same way he did.

* * * * *

COMING NEXT MONTH

Available November 9, 2010

#2047 THE MAVERICK PRINCE
Catherine Mann
Man of the Month

#2048 WEDDING HIS TAKEOVER TARGET
Emilie Rose
Dynasties: The Jarrods

#2049 TEXAS TYCOON'S CHRISTMAS FIANCÉE
Sara Orwig
Stetsons & CEOs

#2050 TO TAME A SHEIKH
Olivia Gates
Pride of Zohayd

#2051 THE BILLIONAIRE'S BRIDAL BID
Emily McKay

#2052 HIGH-SOCIETY SEDUCTION
Maxine Sullivan

SDCNM1010

REQUEST YOUR FREE BOOKS!

2 FREE NOVELS
PLUS 2
FREE GIFTS!

Passionate, Powerful, Provocative!

YES! Please send me 2 FREE Silhouette Desire® novels and my 2 FREE gifts (gifts are worth about $10). After receiving them, if I don't wish to receive any more books, I can return the shipping statement marked "cancel." If I don't cancel, I will receive 6 brand-new novels every month and be billed just $4.05 per book in the U.S. or $4.74 per book in Canada. That's a saving of at least 15% off the cover price! It's quite a bargain! Shipping and handling is just 50¢ per book.* I understand that accepting the 2 free books and gifts places me under no obligation to buy anything. I can always return a shipment and cancel at any time. Even if I never buy another book, the two free books and gifts are mine to keep forever.

225/326 SDN E5QG

Name _____ (PLEASE PRINT)

Address _____ Apt. #

City _____ State/Prov. _____ Zip/Postal Code

Signature (if under 18, a parent or guardian must sign)

Mail to the Silhouette Reader Service:
IN U.S.A.: P.O. Box 1867, Buffalo, NY 14240-1867
IN CANADA: P.O. Box 609, Fort Erie, Ontario L2A 5X3

Not valid for current subscribers to Silhouette Desire books.

Want to try two free books from another line?
Call 1-800-873-8635 or visit www.morefreebooks.com.

* Terms and prices subject to change without notice. Prices do not include applicable taxes. N.Y. residents add applicable sales tax. Canadian residents will be charged applicable provincial taxes and GST. Offer not valid in Quebec. This offer is limited to one order per household. All orders subject to approval. Credit or debit balances in a customer's account(s) may be offset by any other outstanding balance owed by or to the customer. Please allow 4 to 6 weeks for delivery. Offer available while quantities last.

Your Privacy: Silhouette Books is committed to protecting your privacy. Our Privacy Policy is available online at www.eHarlequin.com or upon request from the Reader Service. From time to time we make our lists of customers available to reputable third parties who may have a product or service of interest to you. If you would prefer we not share your name and address, please check here. ☐

Help us get it right—We strive for accurate, respectful and relevant communications. To clarify or modify your communication preferences, visit us at www.ReaderService.com/consumerschoice.

SDES10R

*See below for a sneak peek from
our inspirational line, Love Inspired® Suspense*

Enjoy this heart-stopping excerpt from
RUNNING BLIND
*by top author Shirlee McCoy,
available November 2010!*

**The mission trip to Mexico was supposed to be an
adventure. But the thrill turns sour when Jenna Dougherty
and her roommate Magdalena are kidnapped.**

"It's okay. I'm here to help." The voice was as deep as the
darkness, but Jenna Dougherty didn't believe the lie. She
could do nothing but lie still as hands slid down her arms,
felt the rope around her wrists.

"I'm going to use a knife to cut you free, Jenna. Hold
still."

The cold blade of a knife pressed close to her head before
her gag fell away.

"I—" she started, but her mouth was dry, and she could
do nothing but suck in air.

"Shhh. Whatever needs to be said can be said when
we're out of here." Nick spoke quietly, his hand gentle on
her cheek. There and gone as he sliced through the ropes on
her wrists and ankles.

He pulled her upright. "Come on. We may be on
borrowed time."

"I can't leave my friend," Jenna rasped out.

"There's no one here. Just us."

"She has to be here." Jenna took a step away.

"There's no one here. Let's go before that changes."

"It's dark. Maybe if we find a light…"

"What did you say?"

SHLISEXP1110